THE

Krishna

Marisa had married Cesare Gianelli to get her young brother out of trouble—though it didn't take her long to fall in love with him. But Cesare, it was clear, only wanted her as a housekeeper. Could she ever expect to find happiness with him?

Books you will enjoy
by HELEN BIANCHIN

THE HILLS OF HOME

Mitch Ballantyne had only to beckon and all the girls came running—including his step-sister Shelley! But how Shelley wished her dear stepfather Luke didn't make it so obvious that he would like to see the two of them make a match of it, when it was clear that no such thought had ever crossed Mitch's mind!

AVENGING ANGEL

The only way Terese could save her beloved stepfather from disaster was to marry the forceful Manuel Delgado, a man she hardly knew. And Manuel had made it plain that the marriage would *not* be 'in name only'. How could she go through with it?

BEWILDERED HAVEN

Jenny thought Zachary Benedict was the most conceited man she had ever met, and she had no intention of becoming yet another in his long string of conquests—and anyway, after Max, she didn't want to get involved with *any* man again. But Zachary, for reasons of his own, pursued her relentlessly. Surely she wouldn't find herself weakening?

THE WILLING HEART

BY

HELEN BIANCHIN

MILLS & BOON LIMITED
17–19 FOLEY STREET
LONDON W1A 1DR

First published 1975
Australian copyright 1978
Philippine copyright 1978
This edition 1978

ISBN 0 263 72664 9

Set in Linotype Baskerville 10 pt.

Made and printed in Great Britain by Richard Clay (The Chaucer Press), Ltd., Bungay, Suffolk

CHAPTER ONE

Oh no! Marisa sat in stunned disbelief as the curtly delivered words rang in her ears. A *two*-hundred-dollar fine! The amount was so incredible, she barely registered the magistrate's remaining words as he decreed a twelve-month driver's licence suspension.

It was incorrect, it had to be! With a sense of rising panic she tried desperately to catch the lawyer's eye, but his head was bent as he hurriedly gathered papers into his briefcase.

In a daze, she rose from the long wooden form and made her way alongside several jostling figures all equally intent on vacating the austere courtroom. Voices murmured indistinctly around her as she sought a vacant space along the hard wooden forms stretching side by side down the length of the corridor, for she felt decidedly weak at the knees.

'Miss Maxton.'

She turned to find the lawyer immediately behind her, and the words tumbled out disjointedly as she voiced her incredulity.

'It's not—two hundred dollars, is it?' A stray lock of golden hair fell forward and she smoothed it back behind her ear with a shaky hand. 'I mean—it couldn't be. Not for a first offence, surely?' she implored desperately, her eyes dilating with anxiety. 'You explained——' she faltered as he began to shake his head regretfully.

'I'm sorry, Miss Maxton, really,' he shrugged his shoulders irritably, vaguely disturbed by the earnestness of the young girl facing him. 'Old Quensell is known to be very hard on young lads, particularly those with long hair, and,' he paused imperceptibly, quirking an expressive eyebrow down at her, 'sloppy clothes.'

Again, he shook his head slowly, and continued in a matter-of-fact manner.

'If your brother had had his hair cut, as I advised, and been more conventionally attired, I'm sure the fine would have been considerably less.'

He hesitated a few brief seconds as Marisa eyed him wordlessly. 'If you will wait here, I'll arrange for your brother's release,' he instructed, and turned to stride along the hallway and disappear from sight.

Two hundred dollars. Just like that. A whole year's savings, plus one month's rent, gone in a matter of seconds.

'My brother Tony!' she sighed expressively, raising her eyes heavenward. Divine assistance was never more doubtful!

The sun streamed in on to the dull brown linoleum, and sounds of the outside world made themselves heard as a cargo ship announced its departure with a single sonorous boom from the nearby wharves accompanied by an irate blast of a car-horn and the hair-raising screech of hastily applied brakes. Marisa winced against the inevitable crunch of impact as metals collided and found herself releasing a heartfelt sigh of relief when seconds ticked on by and no sound of a crash reached her ears.

Impatiently she looked down the corridor for Tony, aware that there was no chance of her being able to return to the office in time to do anything other than cover her typewriter. Mr Bennett was bound to be annoyed when she failed to return, and quickly she rose to her feet to go in search of a telephone.

Tony appeared in the corridor minutes after she returned, and she regarded him silently, anger at the result of his careless, irresponsible, childish actions replacing anxiety.

He ambled sheepishly towards her with his hands thrust deep into the pockets of his scruffy denim jeans. His hair, almost as pale as her own, appeared lank and listless and very much in need of a wash.

She couldn't smile, or even speak to him. She didn't trust herself to be civil.

In silence they walked side by side to the Mini, its red paintwork dulled with age and speckled with dust, and Marisa drove it out on to the main highway towards the coast, and Port Douglas, with deliberate efficiency.

Lounging in the seat beside her, Tony reached into his shirt pocket for cigarettes and matches, and at the vexed look on his sister's face, decided silence was the best policy for the moment.

Marisa felt her inner tension ease as they left the outer suburbs of Cairns and branched off towards the Cook highway. Steadily acre upon acre of swaying green-leafed cane emerged on either side as the ribbon of asphalt dipped and curved towards the coast. Narrow train tracks ran alongside the highway to cross and recross the asphalt as each cane farm became linked by a network of tracks that enabled small diesel engines to haul the wagon-loads of cane to the mill.

To the right, several hundred yards from the road in a paddock of burnt-off cane, a group of soot-blackened men wielded their machetes in the heat of the sun. Above them the sky was a clear light blue and the air held a stillness, almost as if all of nature's smallest creatures had paused to listen to some strange infinitesimal sound.

The sea stretched out over the horizon in a glorious expanse of translucent blue, deepening as the ocean floor plummeted into murky obscurity, and Marisa negotiated the many sweeping bends with care as the road followed the coastline for several miles, winding around heavily bush-clad hills fringing the shore.

Neither Marisa nor Tony attempted to speak, each seemingly engrossed with contemplative thoughts they had no wish to share.

She felt an immense feeling of relief as she parked the Mini on the grass-tufted verge in front of the cottage at Port Douglas. It wasn't a modern dwelling, but its weathered wooden structure was endearingly familiar and being built close to the beach lent it an air of peaceful tranquillity. At high tide the water lapped against clumps of spinifex on the edge of their boundary and there were two elderly coconut palm trees only yards from the back steps.

Inside the cottage Tony took a can of beer from the fridge and opened it, thirstily gulping the icy liquid with obvious enjoyment, while Marisa plugged in the electric jug to make a much needed cup of coffee for herself.

Feeling the necessity to say *something*, she schooled her voice into civil tones with determined resolution.

'You'll have to get a job, and soon, Tony,' she began firmly, spooning instant coffee and sugar into a cup. And from now on, you'll just *have* to contribute something towards housekeeping each week.' Her voice shook a little, and he had the grace to look rather ashamed of himself.

'All right, all right,' he mumbled, letting out a sigh of discontent. 'I'll go into the Cane Association's office tomorrow. They always want men this time of year. I'll get something.'

He lifted the beer-can to his lips and drained the remaining liquid in long thirsty gulps.

'Thanks for getting me out,' he muttered, slouching down into the chair as he gazed absently into the framed landscape on the kitchen wall.

Marisa managed a curt nod, not trusting herself to speak. She longed to let loose some of her pent-up anger against him. To scream out—'Why, why, why have you done this? How *could* you be so stupid! Can't you get it through your thick head that if you had worked hard for one year, just one year, between us we could have saved enough money for that last year at college. And if you'd *really* tried hard, you might have won a bursary enabling you to enter medical school. Now you've flung it all away. There's no chance now, no way!'

But she remained silent, biting her lip with frustration, knowing there was no way to reach him any more. Since her father's death two years ago, her one ambition had been to save sufficient money to put Tony through college and medical school. Now, it seemed an unattainable dream!

Tony recognised the tenseness around her mouth,

and with a muttered, 'I'm going for a swim. See you,' hurriedly left the room.

Marisa sat down at the table, the effects of the afternoon's events numbing her into immobility. It was still so vivid in her mind, that terrible argument she had had with Tony just three nights ago. He had consumed can after can of beer, to a point where he hardly knew what he was saying, and she had scolded him angrily, furious that his attitude to life had become so negative. His reactionary fit of temper had been terrible, and he had finally slammed out of the cottage to drive the Mini away at breakneck speed. Halfway to Cairns, a police patrol car had seen him and given chase, finally forcing a halt. His resultant use of foul language combined with resisting arrest for drunken driving had put him behind bars for the weekend. She would never forget that clutch of fear as she opened the door much later that Friday evening to be confronted by a police officer and had been informed of what had happened.

It was quite a while before she summoned sufficient energy to begin preparing something for tea.

Tony came in just as she was dishing up the meal, and she looked at his slender young frame with something akin to vexation.

'Hurry up and change, tea's almost ready.'

'Sure, smells good. I'm famished.'

He had a cheeky face, smooth-skinned and pixieish, with wavy fair hair and bright blue eyes. He was whipcord-lean, this boy/man brother of hers, with a charm and ready wit which endeared him to her, despite his rather belligerent behaviour of late. She knew how he must feel at having his chances knocked out from under him. Seventeen is such an awkward age, she had excused again and again.

During the meal he was eager in his efforts to work hard, to turn over a new leaf. But Marisa listened rather sceptically, as she had heard it all before.

'Where will it all end?' she asked silently, despair settling on her slim shoulders like a tangible weight.

Good as his word, Tony rose early next morning

and accompanied her into Mossman, strolling into the office where she worked just before lunch to tell her he had a job cutting cane on a farm ten miles north of town.

The next few weeks passed smoothly, and Marisa began to relax a little, as she was helping out at the weekends in one of Port Douglas's hotels, anxiously hoping to increase her very meagre bank balance to cope with a few outstanding bills.

It was a complete surprise when Tony arrived one evening during the week, and Marisa couldn't believe her eyes when he walked in through the door.

'Tony, what on earth——?' she began.

'I quit.' He scowled as he viciously kicked a pot plant several feet across the floor, watching as the clay pot toppled and left a spill of earth as it rolled.

He shot her a baleful look as she regarded him silently.

'And don't start. I know everything you're going to say.' He lit a cigarette, thrusting the packet back in his pocket and flicking the dead match into the air.

'Those damn foreigners! Work, work, work. Slashing away at that blasted cane. Yelling and screaming away at me all the time to hurry up. Madmen! It's not decent to work that hard,' he spat out vehemently. 'To hell with the lot of them!'

He strode to the fridge for some beer, found none, and slammed the door none too gently.

Marisa winced involuntarily, hating the violence evident in every taut muscle of his body.

'Don't suppose there's any tea left?' he demanded querulously. 'I'm starving. All I ate out there was spaghetti, night after night, and meat swimming in oil and tomato paste. And bread. I'd give my soul for a decent stew, or one of your pies.' He looked hopefully at his sister from the chair he had just flung himself into, unconsciously rubbing a thumb along his collarbone in a nervous reflex action, and sighed loudly as she extracted a pan from the cupboard

'You'll have to make do with an omelette,' she said

evenly, with remarkable self-control.

He shrugged sourly. 'Better than nothing, I s'pose.'

Striving to cool her exasperation, she queried if he had picked up his pay cheque and felt unaccountably relieved when he nodded, for it wouldn't have surprised her if he had marched off without it.

'Come over to the pub with me afterwards?' he asked restlessly. 'I could do with a bit of life.'

Marisa opened her lips to refuse, to say she hated it there. Hated sipping brandy and ginger-ale supposedly while Tony drank ginger-ale. Except he switched glasses when the barman wasn't looking. She loathed being looked at and sized up by the men, trying to be polite when refusing to let them buy her a drink.

With a sigh of resignation she realised if she did refuse, he would become even more sullen and argumentative. It would be much easier just to go with him.

She served the omelette on to a plate and cut some bread, putting them on the table, and returned to the stove to make fresh coffee.

'All right. I'll have to iron a dress for work tomorrow, first, and tidy myself up a bit.'

Tony shrugged, busy forking food into his mouth with gusto.

'You know, there was this guy, Sergio, there. He ate raw garlic with everything. Phew! You could smell him coming! And wine! They drank it for breakfast, lunch and tea, *and* in between as well. No wonder they worked so damned fast—they're supercharged!' He spooned sugar into his coffee, and stirred it vigorously. 'And womanise! Wow! The stories I heard would——'

'Put curls in my hair, I don't doubt,' she interrupted wryly.

There were several people mingling convivially in the hotel lounge, the piano was tinkling loudly in an effort to be heard over the noise, and there seemed to be a number of men crowding round the bar when they arrived almost half an hour later.

Marisa followed Tony to a table and tried to ignore

the uneasy feeling in the pit of her stomach as inevitably after he'd downed his drink Tony rose to his feet to participate in a game of darts.

'How about a dance?'

She looked up at the middle-aged man who had voiced the question and politely refused.

'A drink, then?'

She shook her head, assuring him she was waiting for her brother, and with a careless shrug he turned and walked away.

Marisa sipped her drink slowly, trying desperately to appear vitally interested in Tony's dart score, and after half an hour the strain was beginning to give her a headache.

It was a relief when he wandered towards her, and rather anxiously she suggested they go. A particularly noisy group of hippie-type characters had wandered in a few minutes before and were talking loudly with arrogant effrontery among themselves. They looked extremely scruffy and dirty, and more than a little inebriated.

One of their number was eyeing Marisa with avid interest, and her consternation quickly changed to horror as she watched him weave his way towards her, his thumbs hooked into the wide leather belt at his hips.

'Hey, doll,' he leered repulsively. 'Come and have a drink with us.'

Marisa looked up and barely repressed a shudder of revulsion. His shoulder-length hair was thick and dark, and he sported the bushiest growth of beard she had ever seen.

'I'm sorry,' she said with belying firmness. 'My brother and I are just leaving.'

He swayed a little, and then snickered.

'Aw, come on, just a teensy-eensy drinkie.' He held his hand out towards her, and slowly measured a few centimetres between his thumb and forefinger. Then he licked his lips and thrust his face closer to hers. 'My pals an' me haven't seen a doll like you in months. Man, are you a cute one!' His eyes gleamed and he ran his tongue over his lips again, putting out a hand to finger her hair.

She felt her face tighten as she unconsciously held her breath.

'Please leave me alone,' she managed after a few paralysing seconds. 'We have to go.'

She stood up, but he moved closer and put an arm round her shoulder. Marisa backed away, looking desperately at Tony, who grabbed her hand in that instant.

'Come on, let's get out of here.'

The bushy-haired character pushed him down into a chair, slurring his words together as he spoke.

'Shut up, pint-size. Baby-doll here's going to have a drink with me.'

Tony scrambled up on to his feet and glared. 'Leave her alone!'

'Yeah? And who says?' He laughed derisively. 'You?' His pals had inched closer and were standing by with waiting expectancy.

Tony clenched his fists, and Marisa looked apprehensive and rather frightened.

The next few seconds were a blur. One minute Tony was standing and the next, he was crashing through chairs to the floor.

Marisa screamed and put her hand to her mouth, her eyes dilating with fright.

A few men who had been peaceably drinking at the bar helped manhandle the belligerent youth and the rest of his pals out on to the street, while Mrs McCormick and Marisa bent anxiously over Tony's inert form. There was a buzz of concern from the people gathered around them, and at Marisa's stricken look of enquiry someone reassured her that the doctor was being fetched.

Tony looked so pale, and so still, he scarcely seemed to be breathing at all, and the blood flowing from a cut to his lip didn't add to his appearance.

It wasn't long before old Doctor Mallory bustled in with his little black bag, screwing up his nose to push his spectacle frames into position. He was, strictly speaking, retired. Yet, as he said often enough, 'I'll be a doctor till the day I die,' and with the nearest resident doctor several miles away in Mossman, he was called mostly in cases of emergency.

He straightened up slowly, grunting and holding his back as he wriggled his nose so his spectacles slid down a little, thus enabling him to view his audience over the top of them.

'Hurummph! Well, what are you all standing around here for?' He allowed his gaze to swing round the room. 'Someone ring for an ambulance from Mossman. This young lad has a couple of cracked ribs and a fractured jaw, if I'm not mistaken.'

At this there were subdued murmurs from a number of concerned onlookers, and Marisa clenched her hands tightly. This was the very end. Oh, Tony, she silently groaned, why did we have to come here tonight?

It took half an hour for the ambulance to arrive, and by that time the hotel had closed its doors for the night.

'Come on, dear,' Mrs McCormick spoke gently as she placed a comforting arm round Marisa's shoulders. 'There's nothing you can do at the hospital. They'll make Tony comfortable, and you can see him tomorrow.' She gave her a motherly hug.

'Now, a nice hot cup of tea, I think,' she said briskly, leading Marisa through to the kitchen. Within minutes the tea was made and two steaming cups were placed on the table, and as Mrs McCormick sat down opposite she viewed Marisa with genuine concern.

'I don't like the idea of you spending the night alone, you've had a nasty shock.' She shook her head as she spoke, worried at the paleness and rather gaunt expression on Marisa's face. 'Stay the night with us, we've a few rooms spare, and I'd feel much happier about you.'

Marisa looked into the nice brown eyes in that kind face, and she could have cried.

'Thank you,' she whispered shakily.

That good lady beamed. 'Good. Now drink your tea

while I get some linen for number five, and when you've finished, come upstairs.'

'Oh, but you haven't finished your tea yet,' Marisa protested, 'and I can make up the bed—really, it's the least I can do. You've been so kind,' she managed a wobbly smile, feeling slightly overwhelmed.

'There, you look better already, your colour's coming back,' there was relief in Mrs McCormick's voice. 'I'll wait while you finish your cuppa, and we'll do the bed together. Then I can see you safely tucked in for the night.'

Marisa slept in spite of herself, she was so tired and weary, and when she rang the hospital next morning the news was fair. As Doc Mallory had diagnosed, Tony's jaw was fractured, and three ribs were cracked. He had spent the night comfortably, she was told, and Marisa pulled a wry face over the telephone. She couldn't imagine anything comfortable about three cracked ribs and a fractured jaw!

She relayed the news to the McCormicks, and they commiserated with her afresh, anxiously offering their assistance should she need it.

It was hard to concentrate on her work that morning, and she was relieved when her lunch-hour arrived and she could visit Tony. It upset her more than a little to see the discomfort he was obviously suffering. His jaw had been wired together, and her heart went out to him. He looked so young and woebegone.

Misfortune seemed to follow more closely than her own shadow, she mused wryly, trying every trick she knew to coax the Mini to splutter to life outside the office at the end of the day. At last, thoroughly exasperated and feeling close to tears, she slid out from behind the wheel and walked to the nearest garage. The mechanic who accompanied her back to the Mini pronounced the battery deader than a dodo after a brief inspection, and Marisa fatalistically delved into her pay-packet to meet the price of a new one.

CHAPTER TWO

THE following weeks progressed uneventfully. Tony was discharged from hospital and it seemed too good to be true when he was offered employment at the local post office. It was undemanding work and ideally suited to his enforced convalescence.

Much to Marisa's relief she had been able to settle a few pressing bills, and she had almost begun to believe their luck was changing for the better.

It was therefore shattering to receive a letter from the Cairns branch of the bank into which she paid rent for the cottage, requesting that she call on Thursday morning at ten o'clock to discuss the rental arrears with a Mr Grieves who was acting on instructions from Mr Gianelli, the landlord.

Thursday morning. That was only three days away.

Fear clutched her heart. She was behind with the rent, but not that much, surely. After all, she had paid the odd week's rent in between the most urgent bills, and she *had* written a note to the bank explaining their financial circumstances fairly briefly.

Hurriedly she extracted the rent book from her bag and checked it anxiously, dismay and disbelief clouding her vision as she calculated an alarming eleven weeks outstanding. Oh no, she groaned dismally as she sat down rather hurriedly in the nearest chair.

Tony wouldn't have any money, at least not enough to make any difference; he almost always managed to spend the entire contents of his pay-packet within a few days of receiving it. He was touchy enough at the moment without adding to it, and another argument with him was the last thing she wanted.

Thursday morning heightened her nervous tension considerably.

Her alarm clock for some unknown mechanical perversity of its own had not rung at all, and she overslept. Of Tony there was no sign and nothing to assure her he had come home during the night. He had ridden into Cairns with a friend on the back of a motor-bike, and immediately she began to fear the worst, visualising a score of equally horrific situations from which she might have to have Tony extricated. There was no time to do anything other than gulp down a cup of coffee and hastily dash from the cottage.

Her hair swung loosely about her shoulders as she reversed the car on to the road and sent it speeding rapidly towards the main highway. It would take the best part of an hour to reach Cairns, and to ease the silence of her solitary drive she switched on the transistor radio. The miles flew swiftly as she competently urged the small car as fast as she dared, cornering the sharper bends at a rather alarming rate. She had just hit a nice straight stretch of road when there was a thud as she ran over something, and within seconds the sickening sound of the rim clunking rhythmically on the road.

'Oh, *damn*!' Marisa groaned decisively as she brought the car to a halt at the side of the road. She slid out and surveyed the rear left wheel with dismay.

'Bother the thing!' she cursed, tears of frustration springing to her eyes. Everything seemed to conspire against her, it surely wasn't her day at all.

She looked up the stretch of road and grimaced ruefully, for at this hour of the morning it would probably be a while before another car appeared.

Sighing, she opened the boot and shifted all the bits and pieces that had accumulated there for some time. The spare tyre proved stubborn, and she managed to get quite dusty before eventually prising it loose. This was only the second time she had had to change a tyre, and she fervently hoped it wouldn't prove too lengthy a process.

The hub cap was loose, now for the jack. That wasn't too difficult, but the nuts were tight, and she wrestled for five minutes before one loosened. She was wrenching at the second nut unsuccessfully, muttering away under her breath, when a deep masculine drawl penetrated her ears.

'Tch, tch, tch, *signorina*! Such language!'

She twisted round, caught the humorous twist of his

mouth, the slightly mocking glint in his eye, and if she hadn't been kneeling, could have stamped her foot at him.

Really! Why did he have to look so—superior!

Inflamed over her feeble effort with the tyre, she almost spat at him.

'Well, don't just stand there grinning. Do something!'

His eyebrows rose a fraction.

'Temper, temper,' he clicked his tongue again as he bent down on his haunches and held out his hand.

Marisa glared at him.

'The wrench, if you please,' he requested, a hint of wry humour in his voice.

She almost threw it at him in fury. Honestly, men!

No wonder she hadn't heard him drive up, she had forgotten to switch off the transistor radio and it was still blaring merrily inside the car.

Idly she watched him deftly remove the remaining nuts. His back tautened and muscles rippled impressively beneath the rib-knit shirt as he manipulated the wheel. His accent intrigued her, slight though it was. Probably Italian, or Yugoslav, she pondered, for he was not dark enough to be Spanish.

She looked away, seeing for the first time his car halted behind hers. It was a Chrysler Charger, dark green in colour, and she couldn't help admiring its sleek powerful lines as it stood gleaming in the sun.

The faint cranking of the jack brought her gaze back. The wheel was on and within a few inches of touching the road. In a matter of minutes he would be on his way and—oh no! She almost groaned aloud. There was no doubt about it, the spare was flatter than a pancake. It just wasn't turning out to be her day at all!

He stood up and regarded her wryly.

'It is a pity you were careless in checking your spare tyre.'

She glared at him resentfully, finding his height and rugged broad-boned frame overpowering as he stood blocking out the sun. Dressed in beige denim trousers and a casual rib-knit shirt of russet-brown, he emanated an aura of dynamic masculinity. She was suddenly utterly aware of her own attire, and somehow the empire-line sleeveless dress of deep coral linen with its demurely scooped neckline *looked* home-made. Lightly starched and freshly ironed, it was quite presentable, but its neatness was now marred somewhat with streaks of dust and grease. She felt hot and sticky, and itched to be able to wash her hands free of the grime from the tyre she had tussled with.

Marisa drew in a deep breath, then expelled it slowly. Now what!

He had jacked the car up again, unscrewed and removed the tyre, and taking both it and the spare over to his car, he slung them into the boot. Then he turned and surveyed her, his dark eyes raking her slightly dishevelled state enigmatically.

'Come. It seems you must accept further my assistance.'

Marisa shot him a doubtful look, unsure whether or not she should go with him and hating the quality of command in his tone.

'I am not the big bad wolf of your imagination, nor,' he paused as he lit a cigarette and exhaled smoke with evident satisfaction, 'do I kidnap little girls.'

Stung by his quizzical appraisal of her indecision, she was goaded sufficiently to tilt her chin at him angrily.

'I am *not* a little girl,' she retorted furiously, drawing herself up to her full height of five feet and two inches.

'Then I suggest you curb your apprehension and allow me to drive you into Cairns. I take it Cairns is your intended destination?' he slanted down at her, his lips twitching with suppressed amusement.

Oh, the indignity of it all! He was *amused*. Really! He was quite the most arrogant self-assured *unsettling* man she had ever met. And he seemed to bring out the worst in her. She couldn't honestly remember being so rude to anyone before in her life!

Mustering her voice into civil tones, she managed to

convey her gratitude with a brief muttered 'thanks', watching resentfully as he locked the Mini before handing over the keys to her.

The luxury of the interior of his car impressed her, and she couldn't help a feeling of reluctant envy as he adjusted the transmission and unleashed the latent power of the large vehicle. Resolutely she made no effort at conversation and barely affirmed when he enquired whether she was going right into the centre of Cairns.

He pulled into one of the larger service stations in town and left the tyres with instructions for them to be ready as soon as possible. When she made to get out of the car he restrained her.

'Where do you have to go? Can I drop you any closer?'

She kept her hand on the door clasp as she turned to face him.

'My appointment is not far from here, I can walk. Thank you,' she added reluctantly.

He shrugged imperceptibly. 'As you wish,' he said coolly, and glanced at his watch. 'Be here in an hour. I'll take you back.' It was a command, not a request, and she eyed him resentfully, determined not to commit herself.

She began walking briskly along the pavement and barely inclined her head at his sketchy salute as he drove away.

There was a rest-room round the corner and she stopped to wash her hands and freshen her make-up, running a comb through her hair, and managing to brush most of the dust from her dress.

It was nearly eleven o'clock when she pushed open the swing doors into the artificial coolness of the bank and reported apologetically to the desk clerk, praying anxiously as she waited that her lateness would not prejudice Mr Grieves. To her utmost relief he proved understanding, even sympathetic, but when it came time to discuss the rent he did not mince his words.

'Miss Maxton, the owner of the cottage, Mr Gianelli, has instructed me to inform you that unless you make good the rental arrears within one month he will have no option but to begin proceedings against you. That will mean you must vacate the cottage and make arrangements to repay the three months' rent,' he elaborated.

As his words sank in she eyed him with dismay, and to her mortification felt the sharp prick of tears. She blinked quickly and bit hard on her lip in an effort for control. She mustn't cry. No matter what happened she wouldn't cry, she told herself fiercely.

Mr Grieves cleared his throat quietly. 'I am indeed sorry, but there is little I can do to help you.' He observed the whiteness of her knuckles as she clenched the arm of the chair. 'There is no possibility you can make up the rent within the month specified, I suppose?' he queried gently.

She shook her head slowly, a dull ache beginning behind her right eye.

'I couldn't possibly do it, even with the extra I earn at weekends,' she finished on an unconsciously pathetic note. The desire to weep constricted her throat, making her speech jerky and incoherent. Dismally she recounted events over the past few months, and from behind his desk Mr Grieves listened without interruption. However, he explained regretfully, the decision was not his.

'Do you think, perhaps—if I contacted him myself?' she queried desperately.

'You could try, Miss Maxton, it could do no harm,' he replied quietly.

Almost numbly she rose, thanked him, and left the bank. With a glance at her watch she saw there was still half an hour to fill in. If the tyres were ready she could hitch a ride and get the wheel on herself. It seemed silly to wait around, and half an hour would make that much difference. Besides, she was in no mood to match words with the owner of that rather splendid car.

Resolutely she walked briskly towards the garage, only to find she must wait as the tyres were not yet ready. She stood hovering for the best part of ten minutes before a young lad dumped them at her feet.

He eyed her sardonically. 'Reckon you won't go far with those under your arm, miss. I thought it was arranged for them and you to be picked up?'

'I haven't time to wait around, thank you. I have to get back to work,' she added crossly, with thinly veiled allusion to Mr—whatever his name was. 'You can send the account to Maxton, care of the Post Office, Port Douglas.'

Marisa stepped out confidently, but after two blocks and several curious glances she had to admit that he was right. She wouldn't go far, for the further she went, the heavier and more awkward they became. It seemed an age before she was able to get a ride, but the driver proved a chivalrous soul and insisted on fixing the wheel into position for her. She deviated towards Port Douglas even though it meant her return to the office would be delayed even further, but a wash and change of clothes were essential.

Brenda looked up as she came in through the office doorway.

'Trouble? You've been gone so long I was beginning to get worried. By the way, your brother rang and said he'd hitched a ride back from Cairns this morning. Old Bennett has popped in and out repeatedly over the last half hour. It might be an idea to get in first, before he does,' she advised.

Marisa sighed and put her bag down beside her desk. Hopefully, if she offered to work late and make up her time off, Mr Bennett wouldn't be too cross, and within a few minutes she emerged from his office having committed herself to finishing a lengthy report.

'How did you go?' Brenda had touched up her make-up and was on her way out to lunch.

Marisa looked up, wrinkled her nose, and smiled slightly. 'Oh, he didn't seem to mind. After all, there was little I could do about it. Brenda, be a dear and bring me back some coffee and a sandwich, I haven't had time to eat. Here,' she handed over some coins from her purse. 'Thanks a million.'

Brenda waved as she slipped out from the office, and

Marisa sat down at her desk and collected the necessary foolscap and carbon, and began typing at full speed. She was a good typist, and apart from pausing for the coffee and sandwich which Brenda brought back for her, her fingers flew over the keys swiftly all afternoon. She determinedly pushed the morning's events to the back of her mind, and was successful until Mr Bennett and Brenda left the office at five o'clock. Then she paused to reflect on the best method of contacting Mr Gianelli. The telephone? Direct contact seemed the ideal solution. If she rang, she could suggest a suitable time to discuss it with him.

She picked up the telephone directory and leafed through it until she found the appropriate exchange, and then searched for Gianelli. Scribbling down the number, she rang the exchange and placed the call. In a few short minutes she was through.

'Yes?' the voice was deep and sounded impatient.

Marisa swallowed, and her voice was a little unsteady as she queried 'Mr Gianelli?'

The voice at the other end intoned an even more impatient '*Si.*'

Oh dear, this wasn't going to be easy.

'Mr Gianelli, this is Marisa Maxton speaking.'

There was silence at the other end.

'I rent the cottage at Port Douglas from you,' she enlightened him further.

'Yes,' the answer was curt.

Oh, bother the man! 'I—that is, Mr Grieves at the bank—suggested I might see you personally. About the rent—I can't pay all the arrears in one month, but I wondered if I could see you—to—to discuss it,' she finished dismally. He obviously wouldn't agree.

'Where are you ringing from?' the deepness of the voice so close to her ear startled her.

'Mossman.'

There was silence for a few seconds.

'You work there?' he queried, and she acquiesced.

'What time do you have lunch?'

She said quickly, 'From one till two o'clock.'

The voice continued. 'Very well, where?'

She swallowed, unsure of his meaning. 'I beg your pardon?'

There came a muffled imprecation. 'Where do you work?'

Marisa clutched the phone. 'Oh, the taxation firm, Bennett and Farquhar,' she said with sudden realisation.

'I know it. One o'clock, then.'

Relieved that the conversation was almost over, she murmured a timid 'yes' and heard a dull click as the receiver was replaced.

What an extraordinary man, and obviously not one to waste words!

The following morning was a flurry of activity, especially as Brenda didn't come in, and Marisa had to attend the telephone and reception desk. Mr Bennett was in a liver over something, and the impending encounter with her landlord wasn't helping Marisa's peace of mind.

Emerging into the outer office a few minutes after one o'clock, she was startled to see the tall broad frame of a man studying the wall map intently.

She coughed gently, and he turned at once.

Good heavens! Oh no, she groaned silently it *couldn't* be. She shut her eyes momentarily, and when she looked again she saw with unconcealed dismay that her eyes had not deceived her. The man facing her was none other than the rugged and rather superior man who had stopped to help her change the tyre the day before.

He didn't seem in the least surprised, in fact when she had time to think about it later she could have sworn he had known who she was all along.

'Miss Maxton.'

Oh dear, there was just a slight chance it wasn't ... 'Mr Gianelli?' the sound of her voice surprised her. She hadn't realised she had spoken aloud.

He nodded briefly, his expression a careful mask of inscrutability. 'Shall we go?' he enquired curtly.

'Go?' Marisa echoed stupidly.

He concealed his impatience with effort. 'As this is

your lunch-hour, I suggest we conduct our discussion over a meal.'

Horror filled her. 'Oh no, I mean——' she hastened to amend, ever conscious of the few cents in her purse. 'I don't eat much for lunch.'

His eyes raked her petite dimensions. 'You don't look as if you eat at all,' he concluded bluntly.

Colour flew to her face, but before she could gather her scattered wits, her arm was taken and she was firmly led out on to the street and put into his car. Within a few minutes she was taken inside the town's largest restaurant and had a meal ordered for her without being able to utter one word in further protest.

Creasing the edge of the tablecloth nervously between her shaky fingers, Marisa began her carefully rehearsed explanation about the rent, managing only to utter a few words before he dismissed it with the injunction that it could wait until after they had eaten.

The meal arrived with an amazing swiftness. Large plates on which reposed a splendidly large succulent T-Bone steak and an assortment of vegetables, steaming aromatically and decidedly mouth-watering.

'I can't——' she began, and was abruptly cut short.

'You have a habit of not doing as you are told, haven't you?' he remonstrated, a glint of anger appearing in those dark eyes, and she knew at once he alluded to her not waiting for him at the garage the previous day.

Silently she picked up her knife and fork and proceeded to do justice to the delicious meal in front of her.

When coffee had been set down on their table and he had lit a cigarette, she tentatively began her request to pay the rental arrears over a period of six months. She'd spent time working out that that was how long it would take.

He listened with apparent patience until she had finished, and the silence grew until after a seemingly endless length of time he broke into speech.

'You have gone to great detail,' his voice and his expression were inscrutable.

Marisa's heart sank despondently. He wasn't going to agree, she just knew it.

Unknown to her, all colour had left her face and the man opposite narrowed his eyes in anger. He chose not to enlighten her that Mr Grieves had already been in touch with him by phone and relayed the interview verbatim and also made a few discreet inquiries through various sources.

His voice, however, was deceptively calm.

'Perhaps you will be good enough to enlighten me as to how the rent managed to get so far behind?'

Marisa swallowed nervously, then with a sense of fatalism her expressive face moved to form a wry smile.

'The reason why, Mr Gianelli, since you obviously will insist upon knowing, is that since my father died two years ago after a long illness, I have been unable through lack of sufficient money to carry the financial burden of putting my brother through college and medical school. He's only seventeen now, and over the last year he's had four different jobs and managed to get caught up with the police once.' She paused, and then continued shakily. 'He's had his licence suspended for driving under the influence of alcohol, and I can't pay the rent because I had to withdraw all my savings to pay a two-hundred-dollar fine almost three months ago to prevent him going to jail. Then there were bills, one after the other. The lawyer, the car, electricity——' she stopped abruptly and fought the tears which threatened to engulf her.

The silence which followed seemed to last a small lifetime, for he finished his cigarette and lit another, smoking the second almost to the butt.

'You feel, perhaps, that because your brother cannot continue with his studies, this is the reason for his—foolishness?'

Her emotions under control, she nodded, looking at him closely for the first time and noting with surprise that his brown eyes were very dark, and his features very strong. He was not a handsome man by any means, but he possessed a ruggedness that was attractive, and an elusive charisma which overwhelmed her. There was a ruthless expression on his broad chiselled features at that moment, and she didn't imagine he would be kind at all.

'Yes, I do, really,' she revealed slowly. 'He's not basically bad, just very—impressionable.' She went on reflectively, 'As long as I can remember he's always wanted to be a doctor, and it's been his burning ambition to specialise in heart surgery. I think he has every newsclipping there is on Dr Christiaan Barnard. There's another surgeon, too, in New Zealand, Barrett-Boyes, I think, whom he admires tremendously. Tony is clever, he studied hard. That is, up until last year,' she faltered, and bent her head, but not before he had glimpsed the quiver at the corner of her lip.

'Come, we will go somewhere quieter,' he suggested curtly, and she rose to her feet and followed him out to the car, sliding obediently into the front seat as he held open the door.

In silence he drove barely a mile before pulling off on to the side of the road.

'If I do agree to let you stay on at the cottage,' he pursued relentlessly, 'what guarantee have I that something else won't happen to strain your financial resources in the six months you say it will take to repay me?'

Whatever gave her the idea he might be approachable? He was an ogre of a man, with no heart at all.

'Then you refuse?' she queried desperately, her disappointment plain to see.

'I have a solution.' His words had effect, for her eyes lit up and she breathed a shuddering sigh of relief.

'Oh, you don't know how grateful I am. I just don't know what we would have done if you had turned us out.'

He extracted a cigarette from his packet and lit it with studied ease.

'My solution does not entail you staying at the cottage.'

His clipped words fell with decisive singleness, like

fire crackers going bang bang bang. They could not have had more effect had they been just that.

Realisation struck, and with a strangled gasp of rage and indignation she reached for the door clasp. He moved quickly and her hand was caught in a bone-crushing grip, and she cried out involuntarily with the pain of it.

He was very close, his head only inches away from hers, and as she looked at him wordlessly, the pain he had inflicted plus the futility of the whole wretched situation showed in her eyes, and one solitary tear spilled slowly down her cheek, coming to rest at the corner of her mouth. She licked it with the tip of her tongue, and with a muttered imprecation he let go of her hand. Taking a large handkerchief from his trouser pocket, he handed it to her, but she shook her head and turned away from him.

She stared sightlessly into the surrounding growth of cane for several minutes, trying to regain her composure. Heavens, she thought desperately, I can't—daren't—cry here. What's the matter with me?

He released a long-drawn-out sigh of impatience.

'You are quick to jump to conclusions—the wrong ones, I assure you,' and he frowned slightly through the haze of cigarette smoke. 'I have a tobacco farm a few miles from Dimbulah, and over the last few years I have had numerous housekeepers. They've left because the work is too hard, the hours too long, and the number of men to cook for, too many. I pay my men well, but they work hard, and they need good food and plenty of it.'

He gazed at her keenly, not particularly enjoying the distress he had caused her.

'Last year, the same problem, and the year before that. It is becoming impossible to run the farm on this basis. I need a wife, and to be honest with you,' he continued calmly, 'I intended writing to my sister in Italy to select a suitable girl for me. It seemed the only solution.' He paused speculatively. 'But now,' his shoulders lifted expressively, 'perhaps I need not trouble her.'

During the last few minutes her eyes had grown wide with disbelief that her ears were hearing what she thought they were.

'If you will consent to be my wife,' he elaborated, 'I will forget about the rent, and I'll undertake the financial arrangements necessary to put your brother through college and medical school.'

CHAPTER THREE

MARISA gasped incredulously. 'You mean, marry you?'

His lips twisted into a wry smile.

'I know of no other way for you to become my wife. Unless, of course,' he drawled, with the hint of a twinkle in his eye, 'you are suggesting a more unconventional arrangement?'

Her eyes widened, and she looked distinctly shocked.

'You can't be serious?' she whispered.

His eyebrows lifted. 'Serious about what? Marriage, or an unconventional arrangement?'

She blushed with confusion, her eyes very bright. 'How can you speak like this? Make arrangements as if we——' she faltered. 'We're strangers,' she burst out at last. 'I don't know you—anything about you.'

He shrugged imperceptibly. 'What do you wish to know? Is it so important? I daresay the eminent Mr Grieves would conduct a formal introduction and reassure you as to my character and financial status, if it bothers you? I am not a poor man, as my wife you will have most things you want.'

She remained silent, scandalised and a little shocked.

He went on quietly. 'In my country, a marriage is still quite often arranged to suit the respective families. Sometimes the couple do not even meet until just before the wedding. The marriages are successful. Why should they not be?' he shrugged slightly. 'This way there is no—what is the expression—rose-tinted spectacles? No illusion to be destroyed afterwards.'

She spluttered into speech. 'You mean, you would just write to Italy, and on your sister's recommendation, marry a girl you'd never met?' Her eyes were large with astonishment. 'What if she proved—well—difficult?'

His expression hardened and took on a ruthless quality. 'There would be no possibility of that happening.'

With sudden clarity, Marisa saw that it wouldn't. He was the type of man who would probably beat his wife into submission. The poor girl would comply with him out of the sheer necessity for a peaceful existence!

'But I don't understand,' a pleading note entered her voice. 'Why can't I pay the arrears off, as I suggested?' Her eyes were large pools of incredulity. 'I mean——'

He interrupted impatiently. 'My terms are the only ones acceptable to me.' The words had an arrogant ring of finality.

Toying with the strap of her shoulder bag, she asked slowly, 'If I did agree to marry you, what—exactly—would you—demand of me?'

His eyes became hooded, his face expressionless.

'Simply, that you look after the house and cook for the workers,' his voice was cool and impersonal.

'That is—all?' The unasked question she could not quite put into words lent an anxious pinched look to her face.

His dark brown eyes bored into her hazel ones with a savage intensity, and his expression became even harder.

'That is all, for the time being,' he spoke very distinctly, adding, 'Our marriage would be a permanent arrangement. I do not hold with divorce. You must understand, *now,* that eventually I will insist you share my bed and bear my children. Think carefully,' he cautioned relentlessly. 'Once you have made your decision, it will be irrevocable.'

Her face had suffused a delicate pink as he spoke, and then become pale and tense. He regarded her speculatively, then continued in a voice that was surprisingly gentle.

'When you've had time to think about it, you'll agree with me.'

The car sprang to life at his touch, and Marisa sat in contemplative silence during the short drive to the office. There was no doubt in her mind Tony needed sorting out, nor any doubt this man could do just that. If only Dad hadn't died when he did—but it was no use wishing. She sighed. To imagine a life not at constant odds with insurmountable debts seemed idyllic.

The car drew in to the pavement, and she put a hand on the door clasp.

'Thank you for lunch,' she felt suddenly shy. He seemed so large and indomitable.

'I'll come to the cottage tonight, about eight. You shall give me your answer then.' He smiled, and she marvelled at the transformation of his hitherto stern countenance. *'Ciao.'*

How she managed to get through the afternoon was a mystery. She typed automatically and answered the phone, her mind only partially concentrating as she feverishly endeavoured to delay giving rational thought to Mr Gianelli's proposal.

Of Tony, there was no sign. Bother him! She needed him for moral support. She didn't exactly relish entertaining Mr Gianelli on her own.

What would he do tonight? Stay just for an hour or so? Or did he intend taking her out? She shrugged obliquely. Perhaps he would go straight away, as soon as she had given him her answer. Dimbulah was several miles further inland from Mareeba, which in itself was over an hour's drive from Port Douglas. Oh well, she thought philosophically, no doubt I'll find out soon enough.

It was like being between the devil and the deep blue sea. Which was worse? On the one hand loomed a belligerent Tony, sinking lower and lower into his well of depression, making life for both of them a misery, and on the other, a chance to see Tony surface and get his dreams realised, and—herself——? No more debts, no Tony to worry about, a future settled and secure.

There was no choice at all, really, she sniffed sadly. No choice at all. Accept Mr Gianelli she must.

At a few minutes to eight she was ready, looking cool in a fuchsia and lilac patterned sleeveless dress of simulated silk caught in at the waist with a tie-belt of the same material. Her hair, freshly washed under the shower, fell loose around her shoulders in a shining cloud of palest honey-gold, and her face held a light dusting of powder and there was the barest trace of colour on her lips.

She felt distinctly nervous as she fingered her hair, twisting it round her fingers, the nerves in her stomach suddenly knotting as she heard a car slow down and turn in towards the cottage.

He was here. In only seconds he would knock at the door.

She breathed in deeply, tensing as she heard his footsteps on the verandah, then she was at the door, opening it, somehow murmuring a greeting, and he was in the lounge, looming much taller and broader than she remembered.

'Please, sit down,' she said indistinctly, not able to look up at him.

Her shyness seemed not to bother him, and he sat in a chair near the window.

'Would you like a drink? I could make some coffee.' Her voice sounded far away, and she restrained from twisting her hands together, which suddenly she seemed not to know what to do with.

His eyes gleamed darkly, and there was a hint of a cynical twist to his slight smile as he indicated coffee would be fine.

She hesitated, then asked if he took it black or white.

'Black, thank you.'

With a nod, she escaped quickly to the kitchen, and he mused that she reminded him of a scared doe, poised for flight in the presence of the hunter, man.

Shakily she took down two cups and saucers, spooned instant coffee into the cups, and then checked that there was water in the electric jug. Undecided whether or not to add biscuits, she dithered for minutes before she decided not, as he wouldn't long have finished dinner. All too quickly the jug boiled, and she poured the water into the cups and carried them carefully into the lounge, wishing desperately she had sufficient savoir faire to carry off the next hour or so.

He accepted his cup from her, and she set down her own, returning to the kitchen to fetch the sugar bowl. He sugared his liberally, then looked over at her, a questioning lift to his eyebrows.

'Well, Marisa?'

She looked at him, then away, feeling embarrassed and insecure.

'Yes. I—yes,' she stammered nervously.

It was impossible to tell how her acceptance affected him, for his expression did not change.

'That is good.'

He took a pack of cigarettes from his pocket and lit one, inhaling the smoke deeply.

Looking frantically for something to say, she began hurriedly, 'I'm sorry Tony is not here. He——' she was about to say he would be in later, but this man would not be fooled easily, and she finished lamely—'I'm not sure when he'll be back.'

He observed her quietly, and Marisa wished fervently he would say something, *anything*, but he smoked the cigarette leisurely, then stubbed it out in the ashtray on the small coffee table beside his chair. He picked up his coffee, and took his time over drinking it.

'You are quite content to leave everything to me? The appropriate college for your brother?' he queried.

'Yes,' she managed at last, looking him straight in the eye.

The die was cast, there was no going back on her word now.

'Very well. I will make all the necessary arrangements on Monday. Are you of age?'

The question surprised her, and she looked startled.

'Yes, I'm twenty-two.'

He nodded briefly, shifting his broad frame slightly.

'I'll need both your and your brother's birth certificates. Do you have them here?'

She confirmed that she did, and as he was obviously expecting her to fetch them she went into her room and took them down from the little tin box she kept on top of the wardrobe.

Marisa silently handed them to him, and he put them carefully into his wallet.

'You will not object to being married in a Catholic church?' he queried further, and she shook her head.

'No, not at all.'

He rose to his feet, apparently well satisfied.

'You will excuse me if I leave now? There is much to be done. Your brother—I shall want to see him when I come Monday evening.'

It was more of an order than a request, and she nodded, following him to the door.

His presence had created quite a strain, and she was relieved that he was going.

With a curt '*Ciao*' he moved quickly to the car, and within seconds was backing it out on to the road. He did not sound the horn, and she could not see if he sketched a wave or not.

Phew! She was glad that was over and done with. The next thing was to inform Tony, *when* he decided to put in an appearance.

She went back into the house and the loneliness of it engulfed her. She looked at her watch, surprised to see it was just after nine o'clock. He had stayed little more than an hour. And tomorrow he would set the wheels in motion that would churn out the pattern of her life.

Marriage. The thought of it shook her equilibrium to its very roots. To such a man as Mr Gianelli, the acquisition of a wife would no doubt mean the smooth running of his household. She would be expected to cook and wash and clean, and to be obedient. The mere thought of thwarting him sent shivers down her spine. She had no desire to unleash his anger, nor did she doubt she would suffer at his hands should she do so.

She collected the cups and saucers, and rinsed them in the sink, then toyed with the idea of reading, but after a few minutes her thoughts wandered and she restlessly put the book down.

Unable to settle, she extracted the ironing board and ironed everything she could lay her hands on that was even slightly creased.

It was well after ten when she tumbled into bed, and much to her surprise she slept until the alarm woke her at seven o'clock next morning.

Hastily she rose and looked in Tony's room, finding to her dismay that he had not come home. Worry creased her forehead, and she could feel the familiar knot of nerves in her stomach.

Where was he? Oh, really, he was just too much, she cursed crossly!

Hurriedly she made her bed, washed and dressed, then made herself some toast and coffee before leaving for work at the hotel. She spent a miserable anxiety-filled weekend, doubly so as Tony failed to put in an appearance, and by Monday morning had still not come home. He rarely told her where he was going, or with whom, or when he might be back. There was nothing else for it but to ring the post office later in the day. He *had* to be home tonight, *and* in time for her to speak to him first.

Marisa spent an anxious morning, relieved only when she managed to speak to Tony on the phone. He was non-committal, but resignedly promised to be home when she got in from work.

There was a build-up of typing, and with the added strain of Brenda still absent with a nasty virus infection, Marisa had a very hectic day. In one way she was not displeased, for she was so busily occupied she had little time to think of anything else.

Tony was not home, and apprehension gripped her. Surely he should be in by now?

She took out some eggs, cheese and tomatoes from the refrigerator. They would have to make do with an omelette again, she hadn't enough money for meat. Thank goodness there were only a few days until pay-day, she enthused mentally, then suddenly realised her number of pay-days was limited. Just *how* soon would Mr Gianelli arrange for their marriage to take place?

The screen door banged, and she looked round to see Tony standing by the table.

'Hi,' she smiled brightly, and indicated the pan. 'I'm afraid it's omelette again.'

He shrugged and made for the fridge, where he took a can of beer and opened it, draining half the contents before leaning against the table. Whatever else he did with his money, he always managed to have a few cans of beer in the fridge, much to Marisa's chagrin.

'Tony, I want to talk to you.'

The empty beer can clanged down on the table, and she jumped at the sudden noise.

'Oh, hell! Not another lecture!' He reached towards the fridge and extracted another can, draining the entire contents before flinging it across the room.

'I'm sick of this one-eyed, two-bit town. No money, no enjoyment. What is there here?' His voice was stumbling over the words, and Marisa knew with sickening certainty that he'd been drinking solidly since he had finished work. He wagged a finger under her nose.

'I'm off—Sydney. Somewhere where there's plenty of action. Not this sleepy, little dot on the map of a place. If you like it so much, you stay here! But not me! Just because you go all drippy over palm trees and beaches, and small country towns, don't expect me to!'

Marisa could feel her temper rising and she battled to remain relatively calm.

'Don't you think I'm sick and tired of scrimping and scraping, too? I hate it,' she said passionately. 'It's not just you who has to do without things. I can't even buy a new lipstick, and I have to use soap instead of shampoo for my hair. *And* go without lunch, most of the time. Just to scrape enough money together, to exist.' She picked up a knife and fork with hands that shook. 'I wish I could just say— "Go, Tony. Go, and to *hell* with you"—but I can't.'

She turned round to face him, speaking earnestly, desperately willing him to listen.

'Tony, be honest with me, truly honest.' Her voice was shaky with emotion. 'If you had the chance of going back to college, and on to med school, would it make any difference? I mean, *if* there was a way, financially, to make it possible. Would you really want to go?'

He finished his mouthful, chewing steadily as her words sank in.

'You don't *need* to ask that question, you already know the answer.' He forked another mouthful into his mouth. 'Why, have you suddenly won Tatts, or something?'

Marisa sighed, then sat down with her plate of food.

'No, not Tatts. Something else. I've met this man—he owns this cottage. He—wants to marry me.' She forced herself to continue. 'He's willing to foot the bill for you to finish college and enter medical school.'

Tony whistled appreciatively. 'Wow, is he for real?'

She nodded, slowly. 'Yes. He's very—considerate. I think it will be the best thing all round.'

He leant across the table, unable to discern much from her careful expression.

'This guy, who is he? What's his name? I mean, you can't have known him long, you haven't been out with anyone that I can remember.' Sudden realization dawned, and he banged the table with his fist.

'You're doing this for me, aren't you? The big sister act, looking after naughty little brother!'

She stood up, shaking with anger.

'All right. Yes! Yes, I am. It doesn't make any difference to you what I say any more, does it? You just go from bad to worse. It scares me, sometimes, to think how you'll end up, it really does. You've changed so much, I can't get through to you. If Dad could see you now, he'd have a fit!'

She banged a fork on the table. 'I'm so tired of all

this—this never knowing what'll happen next. Do you realise that there's almost three months' back rent owing? That by the time we—or rather, I—pay the finance company each month for the car, then petrol, food, there's practically nothing left? I went into Cairns on Monday to see a Mr Grieves at the bank, but the landlord wouldn't wait any longer. He was going to turn us out!'

Marisa glared at him, and Tony had the grace to look ashamed.

'You're sure this guy's on the level?' he questioned doubtfully, and she sat down wearily.

'Yes, I'm sure. He'll be here soon, you'll see for yourself.'

She ate her omelette in silence, and then pushed the plate away, rising to her feet to make coffee for them both.

'What's his name?' Tony queried, his voice openly curious.

'Gianelli. He has a tobacco farm just out of Dimbulah.'

Tony whooped with delight. 'What a break! A chance to go right through med school, and a meal ticket as well. You will do it, won't you?' He looked suddenly anxious. 'You won't back out, or anything?' As she shook her head, he bear-hugged her. 'Thanks, Sis, thanks a million. This is the one thing I want, more than anything else.'

She had no doubt he meant it, and she sighed with resignation.

The leashed purr of Mr Gianelli's car pulling in beside the cottage reached her as she was stroking the brush vigorously through her hair.

Well, the sooner it was over the better, she supposed as she walked through the lounge to the front door.

He seemed to fill the doorway as he stood with the fading evening light behind him, looking very much at ease with a hand thrust casually into his trouser pocket.

'Hello,' Marisa greeted him with quiet reserve.

'Please come in,' and stood aside as he moved past her into the lounge.

'Would you like a drink?' she enquired politely, extremely conscious of the need to observe a modicum of hospitality. 'There's some beer in the fridge.'

'Thank you,' he acquiesced, sitting down in the same chair he had occupied for such a short while the evening before.

Thankfully she escaped to the kitchen where she opened a can of beer and poured it into a glass. Tony was in his room, which was off the kitchen, and she beckoned for him to go with her into the lounge.

With a shrug, he followed her, and she performed the necessary introductions, feeling embarrassed, for she did not know Mr Gianelli's Christian name.

'Cesare,' he disclosed, unperturbed, pronouncing it 'Ches-a-re' with a slight smile as he scrutinised Tony with an unwavering gaze.

Whether or not he found the longish unruly hair distasteful, she couldn't fathom, but she wished one of them would say something—anything. The silence was unnerving.

Tony met his gaze steadily and was the first to speak. 'I expect you want to talk to Marisa. I'll cut out for a while,' he said, glancing at her, but Cesare Gianelli put up a hand.

'No, stay, please. This concerns you as well. There is nothing I wish to say to your sister that you cannot hear.'

He offered Tony a cigarette, lighting it before returning the match to his own.

'Marisa has told you?' he queried, and Tony nodded agreement. 'I've had a busy day,' he enlightened them both. 'There is a college in Brisbane that can take you immediately, Tony. I was fortunate enough to be able to get a syllabus from the convent in Mareeba, and Father O'Reilly spent some time marking various subjects he feels would be beneficial. The college requires that you wear their uniform, and this we will get in Cairns. Your textbooks will be supplied at the college, and I've made arrangements for you to receive a weekly allowance.' He paused, looking reflectively from Tony to Marisa. 'I've also arranged for us to be married in Cairns, this Friday. Tony can then leave on the evening train for Brisbane.'

The colour drained from her face, and her knees felt suddenly weak.

'You had better resign from your job tomorrow,' he continued evenly, 'as we'll need to spend most of Wednesday in Cairns. Tony will have to get his uniform, and I expect you will both have some shopping to do.'

Marisa gasped incredulously, unable to refrain from whispering in disbelief. 'So soon?' She clutched her throat nervously, and he shrugged his shoulders indifferently.

'There is no reason to delay. The tobacco season is well under way, and the sooner this is over and done with, the better.'

'This' was just another business arrangement to him, obviously, Marisa thought rather hysterically.

He stood up, taking in her pallor, the rather desperate look on her face, and—commanded, was the only way she could describe it.

'Come, both of you. We'll have a few drinks at the hotel.'

Together they walked the short distance down the road, and Cesare ordered champagne, imported French champagne at that, and Marisa sipped it without really appreciating it, feeling numbed at the way her life was whirling out of her control. She found conversation difficult, unable to feel at ease, but Cesare didn't appear to notice her discomfiture and encouraged her to talk about herself.

'There's not a great deal to tell, really,' she began hesitantly. 'I was born in New Zealand, but Mum and Dad moved across the Tasman to Perth when Tony was very young. We both went to school there, it's a marvellous place, and I've some wonderfully happy childhood memories of our family there.' Marisa paused briefly, a hint of sadness creeping unbidden into her voice. 'Then, when I was almost twelve years old, Mum was injured in a car crash and died a few weeks later. Dad took it very badly and couldn't settle very well, there seemed to be so much—so many things—to remind him of her, so he decided to sell almost everything and move to Mount Isa. We lived there for almost seven years. Unfortunately his health began to deteriorate, and as he needed specialised treatment we came through to Brisbane. But his heart was already in a very bad way, and he died a year later. The rest you know.'

She had tried to make light of it, but the man opposite had observed the emotion flitting briefly across her expressive features. He made no comment, just leaned back in his chair regarding her through seemingly lazy brown eyes.

Somewhere inside her stomach the butterflies quickened their tempo at the way this tall, large-framed, chisel-featured man seemed to look right through into her soul, as if nothing about her could escape him.

On the other hand, it was remarkable to see the change that had come over Tony. His eyes sparkled with enthusiasm, his voice was bright and his expression eager. There seemed no doubt she had done the right thing as far as he was concerned.

By the time the hotel was ready to close its doors for the night there were two empty bottles of champagne on the table, and Marisa had to own to feeling quite light-headed.

'Goodnight, Marisa,' the twisted smile was in evidence. 'I'll be down about nine, Wednesday morning.'

Without a backward glance he slid into the car and drove off, leaving her standing in the cottage doorway looking slightly bemused.

There was something about him, she shivered involuntarily. Those eyes of his unsettled her, for a start. They had in their depths the same look of a proud untamed animal whose jungle ancestors had acquired to a fine art the instinct to prey, to stalk, and then to pounce. She shivered again, despite herself. Don't be ridiculous, she chided, he's only a man.

Resolutely she shut the door and went into the kitchen.

'So Friday is the big day?' Tony queried, looking up from studying the syllabus he had spread out on the kitchen table.

Marisa nodded absently, mentally wondering what Mr Bennett's reaction would be at having to find another secretary at such short notice. And Brenda would be all agog for any details. Tomorrow was going to be quite a day, one way or another.

'I'm to catch the nine-thirty train out of Cairns on Friday night. I must admit he's really moved fast.'

Marisa silently echoed his sentiment. Cesare Gianelli most certainly had not wasted any time!

Wearily she went to her room, undressed slowly, and slid unaccountably exhausted into bed.

CHAPTER FOUR

SHE waited five minutes after Mr Bennett came into the office before knocking on his door. She dreaded having to tell him, for she knew he would be displeased.

'Come in,' he called, and she nervously entered the room.

'Yes, Miss Maxton, what is it?' He sounded quite testy, and Marisa began in a rush.

'I don't know quite how to tell you, Mr Bennett, but I'm getting married this Friday. It's been—very sudden,' she faltered, blushing at the obvious conclusion he would draw from that remark.

He looked up at her keenly from his desk, managing to look put out at the same time.

'Your personal life is no concern of mine, Miss Maxton. However, you must be aware how inconvenient it is to me, to give such short notice. I would have thought you could have shown more consideration.'

The unfairness of that last remark stung her into

replying, 'I'm sorry, but I didn't know myself until last night.'

He looked thoughtful, and a little contrite. 'I, too, am sorry. You have proved an excellent secretary, and I shall be extremely sorry to see you go. I take it you will want to finish today?'

Marisa acquiesced, adding. 'Of course, I'm quite prepared to work late.' But he waved a hand negligently.

'Quite unnecessary, Brenda will have to cope with anything you can't manage to get completed. May I enquire who the lucky man is?'

She nodded, and said with a smile. 'Of course. His name is Cesare Gianelli, and he has a tobacco farm in Dimbulah.'

Mr Bennett positively beamed at her. 'Cesare Gianelli! I know him quite well. He is of excellent character. I admire your choice.' He noticed her surprise and hastened to explain. 'I follow soccer very closely, you see. It must be all of seven or eight years that Gianelli has played for Mareeba. A fine player, and a good sportsman. I wish you well, Miss Maxton.'

She thanked him rather dazedly and left his office, relieved that that part of it was over. Brenda was next, and she would prove much more inquisitive.

However, she put it off until their morning tea-break, reluctant to parry the barrage of questions that would inevitably follow.

They had sat down together in Marisa's little office, and Brenda was reaching for a second biscuit when Marisa dropped the verbal bombshell.

'Brenda, I'm leaving tonight.'

Brenda dropped the biscuit in her astonishment. 'Come again, did I hear aright?' she gasped.

Marisa nodded, smiling a little.

'Well, come on, *give*! I mean there must be some stupendous reason.' Brenda's pert little face was a study in curiosity.

'I'm getting married on Friday.'

Brenda clapped a hand to her mouth. 'Saints alive! Who is he? How long have you known him? You didn't tell *me* you were going with anyone,' she finished accusingly.

'Oh, Brenda, you're precious, you really are,' Marisa laughed lightheartedly.

'Well, you could have told me.' Brenda looked put out.

'I didn't know myself until last night,' Marisa answered quietly.

Brenda looked excited. 'How romantic! A real proposal! Well, come on, tell me all about him. I'm positively *dying* to know.' She leaned forward eagerly, her chin propped up in one hand and her elbows resting on the desk.

'His name is Cesare Gianelli, and he comes from Dimbulah,' Marisa began, feeling a little like a repeating parrot.

'Yes, well, go on,' Brenda hastened impatiently, forgetting all about her coffee.

'He has a tobacco farm there. He plays soccer,' Marisa faltered, suddenly aware that that was just about all she knew about him.

'What's the rush? I mean—you *know* what I mean,' Brenda elaborated. 'The wedding, this Friday, when he's only just proposed?'

Marisa sipped her coffee, and tried not to feel alarmed at the way her hand was shaking. She held the cup with two hands, and repeated the very words Cesare had used the evening before.

'The tobacco season is well under way, and there's no reason to delay at all.'

'Ah-hah!' Brenda pounced with a knowing smile. 'He's obviously well off, then. How old is he?'

Oh, this was proving difficult. 'Thirty-three,' Marisa offered. That must be close, she thought, he most certainly wasn't in his twenties.

'Is he tall or short?' Brenda queried.

That was easy. 'Tall, very tall.'

Brenda cast her a starry-eyed look. 'I've always dreamed of being swept off my feet by someone much taller than me. It must be wonderful,' she breathed enviously, gazing into space.

Marisa looked away to the pile of papers resting on her desk.

'He's Italian, obviously,' Brenda stated knowingly. 'How long has he been out here?'

'About ten years, I think,' Marisa guessed, surprised that she hadn't given a further thought to Cesare's nationality. She looked at her watch thankfully, for they had easily had their ten-minute break.

'Brenda, I'll have to get on with all this. There's a lot I must do, if I'm to leave things in any sort of order.' Her tone brooked no argument, and, looking slightly dejected, Brenda left the small office for the reception desk.

At lunch-time Marisa took the Mini to a local dealer, and was quite pleased when they offered her a reasonable price. They were also kind enough to arrange for someone to drive her home that evening, and she left feeling well pleased. It was a marvellous feeling depositing the cheque into her account at the bank, and she felt elated when the clerk assured her that a special clearance fee would ensure she could draw on it the following day.

It was all of six o'clock by the time she arrived at the cottage. She gathered her things, thanked the young mechanic for the lift and went inside, stopping in surprise when she saw Tony in the kitchen, the table set and the smell of steak sizzling on the stove.

'Tony, how nice!' she breathed gratefully, setting her bag at one end of the table. She eyed him circumspectly, for he had had his hair cut, not strictly short back and sides, but within the bounds of a respectable hair-cut just the same. Gone, also, was the surly expression usually apparent, and he actually looked really happy for the first time in two years.

She sat down, and drank half of the glass of beer he had poured out for her, and then searched for the sealed envelope Mr Bennett had solemnly handed her just before she left the office. Inside was a full week's wages in cash and a cheque for two weeks' holiday pay. Oh, the darling, she silently thanked him. Financially, all her problems seemed to be resolving themselves.

Tony placed a steaming plate of steak and eggs in front of her, and then sat down opposite with his.

Impulsively, she put some of the cash beside him, and he looked up questioningly.

'I want you to have that, just in case you need it, for any extras, please,' she entreated him, but he handed it back with an emphatic shake of his head.

'No, Sis, I've got some, thanks all the same,' he said firmly. 'Actually, the boss seemed suitably impressed when I gave in my notice and said I was going back to college. Admired my fortitude, turning over a new leaf, and all that. Nearly passed out when he gave me almost a fortnight's wages. I wasn't even counting on the week's pay I was due for.'

Marisa ate well, famished, suddenly realising she hadn't had any lunch. Tony even did the dishes for her. She was amazed, but made no comment except to thank him.

That evening was exhausting, for she sorted through Tony's clothes, and then attacked her own wardrobe. The casual sheath dresses she had run up on the old portable sewing machine would come in handy as house-dresses on the farm. She thought, rather sadly, that her wardrobe was sadly lacking. A new dress in which to be married, lingerie, and perhaps a pair of cork-heeled sandals, were essential.

At times, when she did pause to think about the fact that, two days after tomorrow, she would be a married woman, her brain became so muddled; there was a distinct advisability in keeping well occupied.

It was well after midnight when she tumbled into bed, to sleep soundly until seven, when the alarm pierced her ears.

An hour later she had showered, made the beds, tidied the cottage, and was beginning to cook breakfast. Punctually at nine o'clock Cesare's car pulled in beside the cottage.

'Hi!' Tony called in greeting, waiting at the front door, and Marisa hastily grabbed her shoulder bag and went into the lounge.

Cesare looked across the room at her, a genial smile on his broad chiselled features. She smiled back, the excitement of the day's shopping in front of her made her happy with the whole world. It was so long since she had been able to shop with any pleasure, without having to watch every cent; *nothing* could cloud her day.

The miles flew effortlessly by, and in no time at all they were in the centre of Cairns.

Cesare firmly insisted that she accompany him into a large jeweller's shop for the purchase of her wedding ring, and she fought to hide her astonishment as he calmly bade the assistant display a selection of engagement rings too. Cesare ignored her horrified protests, and she stood, hesitant and uncertain, and unaccountably overwhelmed as he scrutinised a variety of stones and settings. After a few minutes' deliberation, he selected a solitaire diamond delicately set with diamond-chip platinum shoulders on a wide gold band and slipped it on to her finger. It was exquisite, and she held her breath, almost unable to believe she wasn't dreaming when Cesare nodded in agreement with the assistant and without further ado filled out a cheque.

'It's beautiful, Cesare. Thank you.' His name came easily to her lips, and he smiled complacently down at her from his lofty height.

'Wow!' was Tony's comment when he caught sight of the ring on Marisa's finger.

'I think it's more practical if we split up, don't you?' Cesare suggested. 'Tony and I will meet you in the lounge of the hotel, there, on the corner,' he indicated. As she nodded, he continued, 'As near to one o'clock as possible.' He had extracted a slim fold of notes from his wallet as he spoke, and this he now held out to her. 'Marisa, you will take this and get what you need.'

Her eyes widened, and she took an involuntary half-step backwards. 'No. No, I—I couldn't,' she exclaimed hastily. 'I have some money, from selling the Mini, and—and my wages,' she stammered, nervously fingering her hair. 'There's enough to get what Tony and I both need. Please,' she finished desperately, and felt utterly horrified he should contemplate giving her money.

As if to emphasise her indebtedness, the sun's rays caught the splendour of the diamond on her finger, and tiny bursts of dazzling blues and reds sparkled up at her.

'A shopping expedition in Cairns will be out of the question for at least the next three to four months,' Cesare chided her with something akin to vexation, as he frowned down at her formidably. 'You will get everything you need today.'

She still hesitated, a little unsure, then recognising his pertinacity she reluctantly accepted it, pushing the offending fold into her purse.

'Thank you,' she said dubiously, her face tingeing a delicate pink, and he viewed her with wry amusement.

'One o'clock, then,' he reminded her as they parted.

Marisa spent the next two hours happily exploring the city's boutiques and trying on clothes. Now that the amount on the price-tags was unimportant, the selection was tremendous. Among her purchases was a ravishing full-length nightgown, together with a matching negligée. It was strictly a concoction that dreams were made of, and she had fallen in love with it the minute she had seen it. Of deep coral pink with exquisite lace, it had an absolutely voluminous yardage of sheer and opaque nylon falling all the way down to the floor. It was her one concession to frivolity, and in spite of its ruinously expensive label she possessed no regret at the impulse which prompted her to buy it.

No matter what circumstances had precipitated this marriage, it *was* her wedding day, and Marisa was determined not to make do with just *any* suitable dress. It must be white as they were to be married in church, and finally she saw what she wanted. It was crêpe, a polyester crêpe of snowy white, with guipure lace fitting over the bosom under which the crêpe flared gently to a hemline resting an inch above the knee. It had a demure scooped neckline, with three-quarter length sleeves in guipure lace gently flaring out beneath the elbow. It was exactly *right* and fitted perfectly. She purchased a fine net square with a lace edging to place over her hair, and selected a lovely artificial posy of lily of the valley for her bouquet.

Cesare and Tony were already seated in the hotel lounge, with drinks in their hands, and she walked over to them, a happy smile on her face.

'Well, well. You have done some shopping,' commented Cesare with a ready smile as he strode forward and relieved her of most of her parcels. He beckoned the waiter and ordered her a drink, then indicated he would stow her parcels in the car.

When he returned Marisa and Tony were talking animatedly, and Cesare's eyes softened as they admired her glowing skin and sparkling eyes. She was a very attractive-looking girl, all the more so for her apparent unawareness of it. Slightly below medium height, she was slim, with vibrant honey-blonde hair falling below her shoulders and lovely tawny-hazel eyes which deepened in colour at night. He found them utterly fascinating.

'I've had the most super morning, really terrific!' she exclaimed, unable to subdue her excitement at having so much money at her disposal.

Tony chuckled. 'I hope you've left *some* clothes in the shops! By the look of it, between us, we've just about cleaned them out.'

Marisa looked dubiously at Cesare, at once intimidated by his solemn expression.

'Perhaps I shouldn't——' she began hesitantly, but he interrupted before she could finish.

'I assure you I meant every word when I told you to get whatever you need. As I have already said, I am not a poor man.'

Marisa felt a twinge of uneasiness in the pit of her stomach. After all, what he had spent today, on both herself and Tony, would be little more than perhaps six months' salary for a housekeeper. He had said he paid his workers well, but that he also expected good service in return. She only prayed she could cope. Not only with the copious meals and chores, but when the time came, she hoped she could cope with her emotions where he was concerned.

Lunch was a relaxed and friendly meal, for Tony was exultant at returning to college and provided sparkling repartee throughout. Cesare seemed wholly relaxed, and when he laughed at Tony's wry humour she marvelled at the difference it made. He appeared human, and—yes, *nice*.

As Cesare and Tony became involved in a discussion on the merits of soccer as opposed to rugger, Marisa let her mind slip to the Italian recipe book reposing somewhere in among her purchases. It contained a vast accumulation of recipes and was colourfully illustrated. It was probably going to be her best friend and ally if it did but know it, she mused humorously.

'I've got my ticket for the train. It leaves at nine-thirty Friday evening, and gets into Brisbane on Sunday,' Tony enthused. 'I can't wait to get there and get stuck into my studies. I won't disappoint you, either of you, for giving me this chance. Thank you,' he said quietly, turning to Cesare.

It was quite a speech for Tony, and Marisa felt the prick of tears in her eyes and she blinked hard to control them.

Cesare lit up the inevitable cigarette, exhaling the smoke with obvious enjoyment. 'Well, we've just about wrapped it up, Tony. Have you anything else you want to get?' he queried of Marisa.

'No, thank you,' she assured him politely.

'About Friday,' he began. 'My share-farmer, Carlo Rossini, will collect you both in the afternoon and bring you to Cairns. The service is to be at four-thirty, which will give us plenty of time for dinner at the hotel and a few drinks before getting Tony off on the train.' He paused, and turned towards Marisa as he continued. 'We'll stay overnight in Cairns, and take the morning launch to Green Island for the weekend. It will be a short visit, I'm afraid, as we must be back in Dimbulah on Sunday evening.'

Marisa flashed him a startled look and met his

thoughtful gaze resting on her, and hastily resumed sipping her coffee.

Unexpectedly she found herself a few minutes later with the opportunity of viewing Cesare unnoticed. The hand that held the cigarette was broad, the fingers square-tipped, and she watched in fascination as he inhaled the smoke leisurely. His thick brown hair was well groomed, and waved down on to his neck. The breadth of his shoulders beneath the deep mulberry-coloured knit-shirt intimidated her, and she wondered what it would be like to be held in his arms close against that broad expanse of chest, and shivered, a sudden treacherous weakness assailing her limbs. Almost as if he could feel her eyes on him, he turned slightly, and those dark eyes twinkled wickedly across the table at her. Confused colour rushed ingloriously to her cheeks. Bother the man, she was willing to swear he could read her mind!

'I think, perhaps, we should get on our way. It will take a while to sort all those parcels, and I am expected in Dimbulah for dinner.'

CHAPTER FIVE

WELL, Marisa thought nervously, she was as ready now as she would ever be. She viewed her reflection in the mirror and grimaced ruefully. The pale, wide-eyed, anxious face blinked back at her, looking the antithesis of a bride-to-be an hour before her wedding.

'Come on, Sis, we're waiting for you!' Tony looked in, resplendent in a new suit and looking older than his seventeen years. He dropped a brotherly peck on her cheek and smiled. 'You look smashing. Here,' he thrust a small package into her hand, and moved rapidly out of the room.

She undid the wrapping-paper with shaking fingers, aware of the sound of voices chatting companionably as Tony and Carlo stowed suitcases into the station-wagon. A small phial of Carven's 'Ma Griffe' perfume emerged from its shiny cardboard box and, enchanted, she unscrewed the lid and applied it generously behind her ears, on each wrist and between the curves of her bosom, loving its witching fragrance. Tony's voice urged her to hurry, and she hastily gathered her posy and spared a hurried glance round the room before leaving the cottage.

Carlo Rossini was dark-haired, dark-skinned, and sported a luxuriant moustache. His face creased into a friendly smile as he shook her hand.

''Allo, pleased to meet you,' he expressed in greeting, and his dark eyes shone with pleasure.

Marisa smiled back, genuinely liking him on sight.

'That is everything, yes?'

Tony grinned. 'It had better be, Carlo. Any more, and it would have to go on the roof!'

Carlo laughed, and held open the rear door for Marisa to sit in solitary comfort.

'Okay, we go now.'

And go they did, swiftly and surely, the large station-wagon eating up the miles with ease. They entered the outskirts of Cairns with five minutes to spare, and as they neared the church, Marisa strove against a strong desire to escape. Doubts assailed her senses, doubts so frightening and awesome, the blood throbbed at her temples and she felt the alarming prickle of faintness begin to engulf her. The station-wagon slowed as it turned in off the road and parked behind Cesare's car. Marisa drew in a deep breath as Tony held open her door, and stepped out on to the pathway clutching her posy with trembling fingers.

'Good luck!' With a grin Carlo left them and went quickly down the side of the church.

'Oh, Tony, I'm scared,' she turned an anxious face towards him, forgetting to be strong and elder sister-ish in her need for reassurance.

'Don't be, kiddo. You'll be jake,' Tony bade her in a jolly fashion as he led her into the vestibule. At a nod from the verger he gave her hand a gentle tug, and they walked together down the long aisle to the altar. Marisa's stomach felt as if it was tied in knots as they drew closer to Cesare's dark-suited, elegantly tailored figure, standing so tall and broad, and she clutched Tony's hand desperately, afraid to let it go. He gave her hand a reassuring squeeze as they reached the altar, then relinquished his hold and stood slightly away from her.

For one mad, wildly pounding second she had the desire to turn and run, but at that very moment Cesare caught her hand in his, firmly imprisoning her to his side, and she stood there beside him, immeasurably shy and apprehensive.

The priest smiled on them benignly, and began intoning the words of the marriage service. He had a beautiful voice, so rich and full of meaning, as he recited the well-known lines, and Marisa took them so much to heart she felt like weeping. When it came time for her to pledge her vows, she was almost inarticulate, and barely managed to get the words out in a strangled whisper.

It was all over. She was now Marisa Gianelli.

Her eyes flew open wide as Cesare bent down and kissed her lightly on the mouth, and immediately a delicate pink tinged her cheeks.

Tony kissed her resoundingly, Carlo pumped her hand and placed a discreet peck on her cheek, and to her surprise, as Carlo stepped aside, Mr Grieves stepped forward to clasp her hand warmly.

'Are you feeling unwell?' Cesare questioned from inside the car, frowning slightly at her pallor.

She looked across at him, faintly surprised. 'No—no, I'm fine,' she answered, forcing a smile. She sat, tensed, as his eyes swept over her face with a raking scrutiny, then breathed an inaudible sigh of relief as he eased the car out on to the road.

At the hotel, Marisa ate a little of each course of the meal, and hoped no one would notice. The anticlimax of the past few days was beginning to tell on her, and she was feeling distinctly ill at ease, having serious doubts as to whether or not she had done the right thing by herself. About Tony she had no reservations, but suddenly, the effect her marriage would have was beginning to bother her. It seemed as if she was standing off from afar, quite detached from the small group. 'I'm so mixed up,' she thought despondently, 'and so sad Tony's going, and I wish——' Oh, what *did* she wish? What *more* could she wish for than this? The start of a new beginning for Tony, one that she knew would eventually blossom into the culmination of his dreams. 'Come down to earth, my girl,' she mentally chastised herself severely. 'You can't have your cake and eat it too.'

She forced herself to smile, in between sipping champagne and slipping forkfuls of food into her mouth at very slow intervals, and somehow managed to get through the ensuing two hours.

As they left the hotel, Tony and Carlo showered them with handfuls of confetti, laughing with delight that their premeditated conspiracy had come as a complete and unexpected surprise.

'Oh!' she exclaimed, brushing it off her dress and laughing as it fell on to her shoes and spilt on to the pavement. Cesare chuckled as he shook it off his suit and then lifted a casual hand to her hair. She stood breathlessly still as he picked out several minute pieces, dreadfully aware of his disturbing closeness.

At the railway station there was little time for much conversation.

'Please write, Tony, once a week—promise?' she pleaded desperately.

'Promise, cross my heart. You, too.' He looked awkwardly from Marisa to Cesare. 'Look after her,' he muttered to Cesare.

'I intend to,' Cesare replied solemnly, slapping a hand on Tony's shoulder.

'Send me a postcard from Green Island,' Tony shouted through the open window of the carriage as the whistle blew, and she nodded numbly, forcing back tears as the train slowly chuffed out from the station, waving until it rounded the bend and Tony was out of sight.

Cesare took her arm as he led her back to the car, his

eyes narrowing slightly as he noted how pale and tense she had become.

'I've booked into a motel on the Esplanade. We'll go there now, change, and go somewhere for a few drinks.'

Marisa nodded, her voice barely audible as she said, 'Yes, all right.'

Their suite at the motel was large and luxurious, and she felt immeasurably relieved when Cesare indicated that he intended sleeping on one of the divans in the lounge, leaving the bedroom free for her.

'I'll take the bathroom,' Cesare said over his shoulder as he bent over his case, unclasping it and removing a selection of clothes.

Marisa hurried into the bedroom and discreetly closed the door. Feeling slightly more at ease, she quickly shed her dress and slip, plucked a pair of white crimplene slacks from her suitcase and stepped into them, then pulled on a skinny-rib short-sleeved jumper of jade green. She slipped her feet into smart cork-heeled sandals and crossed over to the dressing-table to effect repairs to her make-up.

Heavens, did that pale face with the huge dark eyes belong to her? She looked positively wraith-like, and was vexedly rubbing her cheeks in an effort to restore a vestige of colour when there was a rap at her door and she turned to see it swing open, revealing Cesare in the doorway.

She couldn't stop the startled look that appeared on her face, nor the unsteadiness of her voice as she spoke. 'I'm—almost ready.'

He had changed into hip-hugging fawn suede trousers, with a short-sleeved navy knit-shirt open at the neck. He looked intensely masculine as he stood waiting for her, watching through half-closed eyes as she took unnecessary time fixing stray pieces of hair.

'Would you prefer to have coffee, or something cool?' he questioned from behind her, and looking up, she caught his quizzical glance in the mirror. Feeling the colour rise, she bent and concentrated on replacing her make-up into its case.

'A cool drink would be lovely, thank you,' she said

indistinctly. With a last-minute glance in the mirror she turned and followed him outside, feeling dwarfed by his tall frame at her side as they strolled along the Esplanade and down towards the centre of town.

In the hotel lounge, Cesare led her to a table and ordered drinks from a hovering waiter. Sitting down opposite her, he withdrew his cigarettes and lit one, inhaling deeply before expelling the smoke over his shoulder.

'When we get back from the Island on Sunday evening there will be a belated wedding party at the Dimbulah Hall. It will give you an opportunity to meet my friends, and for them to meet you. Everyone is too busy at this time of year,' he went on to elaborate, 'to get down to Cairns.'

She said quietly, 'That will be nice,' and sipped her shandy.

There was a long silence, and she thrust herself headlong into making polite conversation.

'Would you mind telling me something about yourself, Cesare?' She looked at him apologetically, feeling dreadfully embarrassed. 'I really know very little, apart from the fact that you play soccer, and have a tobacco farm.'

He regarded her lazily, a slow smile tugging his lips. 'Of course. Ask away.'

'Oh, it's things like—which part of Italy you come from, how long you've been in Australia, do you have any family?' she asked, watching as he shifted position with ease, moving one leg over the other.

'Trieste, right in the north, is my town. I left there fifteen years ago, at the age of nineteen, and I have only my parents and one younger sister, Isabella, who is married with four children. She lives in the city, but my parents are still on the farm. Is there anything else you wish to know?'

Marisa shook her head quickly. 'Oh no, that's fine, thank you,' feeling bold at even asking for information, and to hide her unease she sipped her shandy with concentrated effort.

'There is a soccer tournament in Ingham next weekend among the Far North Queensland teams for the Grazioli Shield. We'll leave mid-morning, Friday.' He stubbed out the butt of his cigarette in the ashtray, and drained the contents of his glass quickly. 'A friend of mine is drinking at the bar. You won't mind if I leave you for a few minutes?'

Assuring him earnestly that she didn't in the least mind, she relaxed visibly, glad to be without his disturbing presence for a while.

Half an hour later they were back at their motel, and inside the suite Marisa beat a hasty retreat to her room, murmuring an inarticulate plea of tiredness. As she quietly closed the bedroom door she detected a hint of wry amusement in Cesare's voice as he bade her goodnight.

There were already quite a few people seated aboard the launch when they arrived at the jetty at ten minutes to nine the next morning, and Marisa followed Cesare's tall figure towards the stern. Sitting opposite were a group of American tourists, all relatively elderly, and Marisa wondered if it was her imagination that they were glancing her way in a knowing suspicious way. Was it so obvious that she and Cesare were newly married? She thought not, for although Cesare was courteously attentive, they scarcely presented themselves as a loving couple.

The launch was filling rapidly, and a short while later its engines accelerated to a higher pitch, announcing their imminent departure.

Green Island, Cesare informed her, was a true coral island covered by tropical vegetation comprising thirty-two acres only four feet above sea level, and was sixteen miles to the east of Cairns.

The sea was a glorious green, appearing translucent as the bow of the launch cut its path across the smooth surface. A slight breeze whipped the churning water from the propellers into a light spray, tanging salt into the warm clean air about them, and Marisa compulsively breathed deep of its sweet freshness.

As they neared the long wharf jutting way out from

the small island, Marisa scanned the foreshore with avid interest. Even from this distance it appeared to be exactly as she had imagined a tiny tropical island to be, with an abundance of lush green shrubbery, palm trees with widespread fronds lifting gently in the breeze, sparkling white sand, and almost totally enclosed by a coral reef. She took Cesare's hand, almost without thinking, as he offered it to assist her in alighting from the launch, and a warm ready smile lit up her face as they walked the wooden-planked wharf towards the island. There, it seemed to pulsate with life, and she looked around in wonder that on so small an island there was such an ultra-modern hotel. 'Coral Cay', the hanging wooden sign proclaimed, and when they were shown to their unit she felt slightly in awe of the luxury surrounding her, at the same time breathing an inaudible sigh of relief at the sight of *two* single beds.

A private patio leading off from their room through glass doors captivated her interest, and she wandered across to explore the view outside.

'How about a walk before lunch?' Cesare's voice caught her attention, and she turned back to him, her eyes lighting with pleasure.

'Could we? It looks such a lovely place,' she enthused, and seconds later strove to hide her surprise and confusion as he draped a hard muscular arm across her shoulders.

'Come, we shall satisfy your curiosity with a tour of inspection,' he smiled down at her warmly.

The island unfolded its unique charm, revealing an atoll paradise so enchanting Marisa almost reached out to the elusive, seemingly magical air embracing them. She hadn't seen anything like it, and smiling she turned to Cesare, looking up at him, delight mirrored in her sparkling eyes.

'What a terrific place! Have you been here often?'

He smiled down at her, his eyes crinkling with gentle amusement. 'A few times. It seems to change, something new gets added, but despite that, it is one of the most restful, relaxing places I've ever visited.'

The white sand was deep and crunchy beneath their feet as they walked, and Marisa strained an ear to the soft rustling, whispering breeze moving gently through the leaves, her imagination likening it to a gentle plaintive South Seas lament of long ago.

After an informal lunch they spent the afternoon visiting the Marineland, seeing the live coral and tropical fish, and then boarded one of the glass-bottomed boats. Marisa was enthralled with everything she saw, it seemed incredible that nature alone was responsible for such beauty.

Marisa gathered her clothes together with carefully contrived casual movements, hoping Cesare wouldn't notice she was taking *all* of the clothes she intended wearing to dinner into the bathroom, and it was perhaps as well she did not catch the slight smile on his lips. When she emerged a while later he was sitting in a chair with the newspaper spread out in front of him, and she stood hesitantly uncertain whether the long floral-patterned skirt and sleeveless top were too formal to wear into the dining-room. Cesare's slow wide appreciative smile did strange things to her breathing, and she bit her lip crossly as her cheeks grew warm with tell-tale confusion.

Seated at their table, Cesare suggested she try an entrée of shellfish with grilled barramundi to follow, and ordered a bottle of chilled Sauternes. Mmmn, it was superb, the barramundi was quite the best fish she had ever tasted, and she declined the sweet, settling for coffee. The sparkling chatter all around them lent the atmosphere a gay carefree air, and Marisa found no difficulty in joining with Cesare to converse with several tourists seemingly intent on introducing themselves to as many people as possible. In such a relaxed and friendly fashion addresses were exchanged, and Marisa had no doubt many lasting friendships were begun.

There was dancing in the lounge, and she smiled happily as Cesare led her among the twisting, gyrating crowd. Somehow she hadn't been able to visualise his well-built frame swaying to beat music at all! He had the look of his Roman ancestors, carrying his height proudly, and it took little imagination to see him as a centurion in days long gone. She thought, with a sudden flash of humour, that they must look quite a pair—he so tall and broad, and she easily thirteen inches the shorter!

'I think,' murmured Cesare, some time later, 'it's time we packed it in for the night. Come, you must be tired.' He smiled down at her gently, and as they walked towards their unit took hold of her hand.

He unlocked their door and switched on the light, gently pushing her inside the room. She stood hesitantly beneath the pool of light, pale and apprehensive as she tried desperately to control her thudding heartbeats.

'Get into bed, little one,' he commanded quietly, tweaking back a stray lock of hair behind her ear. 'I wish to enjoy a cigarette in the cool night air.' He bent and brushed the top of her head with his lips. 'Sleep well,' he bade her softly with a smile, then stepped outside, pulling the door closed behind him.

CHAPTER SIX

SHE must have slept almost as soon as her head had touched the pillow, for when she stirred into wakefulness light was streaming into the room and warm fingers of the sun's rays touched on to the carpeted floor. Realisation dawned at the unfamiliarity of her surroundings, and Marisa hastily raised herself on one elbow to gaze apprehensively at the other bed. It had been slept in, for the covers were thrown back and the pillow held an indentation. Immediately she was besieged with visions of sleeping with her mouth open, or worse still, snoring, then dismissed such alarming thoughts, sure that Tony would scathingly have referred to such a lapse if she had ever been guilty of either.

Rising quickly, she showered and dressed, wondering where Cesare could be as the suite was empty, and stifled a startled gasp when he appeared through the ranch-sliders from the terrace.

'Oh, you gave me a fright!' she exclaimed, her eyes widening as her hand flew to her hair. It was hanging loose about her shoulders, and with her face freshly scrubbed and shiny, she looked little more than a schoolgirl.

He took his time gazing at her from across the room, a lazy expression in those deep brown eyes.

'Good morning,' he smiled then, moving into the room. 'I ordered breakfast when I heard you moving around, it should be here soon. Did you sleep well?' he queried, his lips twisting wryly as a delicate pink tinged her cheeks.

'Yes, thank you. And you?' she answered politely, keeping her eyes averted.

'Very well,' he replied blandly, thrusting a hand into his trouser pocket for the inevitable packet of cigarettes. Marisa murmured indistinctly the need to tidy her hair, and set the brush stroking vigorously through the damp curling strands.

'On the patio, I think,' Cesare indicated, when a few moments later there was a discreet knock at the door and a waitress wheeled in a trolley. The girl nodded her approval and continued through the room.

Marisa sat down at the table and poured two cups of coffee from the large silver pot, passing one cup across to Cesare, and selecting a slice of toast for herself. He ate quickly and with evident enjoyment, and Marisa eyed him surreptitiously as she sipped her coffee. She felt slightly more at ease with him this morning, and she idly contemplated what he planned for the day. The sparkling green water not too many yards away looked distinctly inviting, and, oh, it would be so *nice*, just to lie in the sun and laze a few hours away. It seemed an age since she had sunbathed, and she sighed pleasurably at the very idea of it.

'Finished? Like the newspaper?' The query was accompanied with a quizzical gleam, and she shook her head.

'The underwater observatory first, I think, then we'll visit the theatre for the screening of an underwater film. After that,' he smiled across at her, 'you can have your swim.'

She mentally shook her head as she applied moisturising cream, powder and lipstick, trying to analyse why her stomach flipped every time he looked at her. 'Tomorrow will follow today, inevitably, and in spite of me,' she informed her reflection in the mirror.

The sound of Cesare's voice jolted her. 'Ready?'

Quickly she grabbed up a handkerchief and her purse. 'Coming,' she breathed steadily, joining him.

As they made their way towards the entrance down into the underwater observatory there seemed to be quite a few people with the same idea, and in the confined space she felt shy and very much aware of him standing so close beside her.

The tropical fish and coral were truly a thing of beauty in an ever-changing scene. She marvelled that nature could produce such vivid colours in such symmetry, and she gazed through the glass, utterly enchanted.

Once back at the hotel Marisa needed no second bidding to change into her bikini for a swim, and slung a towelling-robe across her shoulders and picked up her sun-glasses before following Cesare down on to the beach. The sand was hot beneath her feet, and she wasted no time in discarding her robe and racing into the water.

It was absolutely gorgeous, so fresh and cool, and she contented herself with a few strokes, then turned on her back and floated, revelling in the feel of the sun on her limbs. With a nimble twist she turned and swam back towards the beach, drying herself off before stretching out face down on the towel. Mmmn, that sun was lovely, she could feel its warmth seeping into her bones, almost.

Cesare was smoking, intently absorbed in an Italian magazine, and she closed her eyes and relaxed. The music from a nearby transistor lulled her into a state of inertia, and she must have dozed for a while, for she woke to the sound of children's quarrelling voices, and lazily raised her head. A short distance away a little boy of about three years was trying to wrench a plastic bucket away from a little tot of not more than two. They were obviously brother and sister, for they had the same fair curly hair and stocky build. She smiled gently as their mother came up to them, scolding severely, to lead them away loudly protesting and almost in tears.

Cesare picked up a plastic bottle of sunscreen cream. 'Here, you'd better use some of this, or you'll burn.' He leant towards her, his eyes inscrutable behind dark glasses. Marisa took it from him, murmuring thanks, sitting up as she unscrewed the bottle and began smoothing the cream over her legs and arms, across the top of her bosom, and midriff.

'Turn around,' he instructed, taking the bottle from her startled fingers. His touch was firm as he smoothed the white creamy lotion evenly across her shoulders, and her stomach flipped alarmingly as he undid her bikini bra and fastened it seconds later. The colour rushed to her face as she contemplated the undoubted expertise with which his fingers had manipulated the clip-fastener. Suddenly cross with herself, she dug into the sand, lifting up handfuls of the tiny grains and allowing them to trickle through her fingers. She deliberated absently on the umpteen women he had undoubtedly seduced, and felt a treacherous yearning pluck at her heartstrings.

'Come on, lazy-bones,' he chided gently, and stood to his feet with an easy litheness. 'We'll have lunch on the patio.'

Obediently she grasped his hand, and was pulled to her feet and led back to the hotel. The glass doors on to the patio glided open at her touch, and she sat down in a canvas chair, turning her face to the sun. Cesare came through a few minutes later with two cans of beer, and she accepted one gratefully.

'Mmmn, that's icy,' she said appreciatively.

Their lunch arrived a short while later and they both ate hungrily off the large plates of sliced cold meats and assorted salads, munching the crunchy bread rolls with relish. Washed down with more beer, it was one of the most enjoyable meals she could remember.

'I'm so glad you brought me here,' she voiced her gratitude with a shy smile. 'It's glorious.'

He gave her a slow, lazy smile as he sat back from the table. 'We'll come back again at the end of the tobacco season, if you like it so much.' He picked up a packet of cigarettes and lit one, inhaling the smoke with enjoyment, and she smiled. He quirked an enquiring eyebrow, and she hastened to explain.

'You smoke an awful lot, I mean you—I'm sorry, I didn't mean to be rude,' she attempted shakily, 'it's just that I saw the humour in you growing tobacco and smoking so much of it,' she paused in dismay, wondering if she had put her foot in it, and offended him. 'I don't mind—I mean, I wouldn't—wasn't——' she hurriedly corrected herself, stumbling on, 'trying to say I don't like cigarettes, or anything,' she finished pathetically, wishing she had never begun on the subject. He must think the sun had affected her, or perhaps the beer had gone to her head!

To her surprise, he threw back his head and laughed.

'Come on,' he chuckled deeply, regarding her with amusement from dark twinkling eyes. 'We'll stroll round the island, then visit the shopping centre and select a few souvenirs. The launch leaves shortly after three.'

All too soon the time of departure drew near, and Marisa felt regretful that they could not stay longer. There seemed to be an elusive magic about the place which touched everyone who set foot on its shore. She had changed into scarlet denim flared slacks with white saddle-stitching on the side seams, and a white sleeveless skinny-rib top. Her hair was caught at each side of her face with kinky wooden slides.

Most of the passengers were subdued as they boarded the launch, perhaps because tomorrow was Monday and spelt back to work for most of them.

In a few hours she would be at the farm, and now it was so near, she hoped she could cope with the cooking and numerous chores. She was an adequate cook, having had plenty of practice during the ten years that had passed since her mother died, and as the launch ploughed through the translucent green waters towards the mainland, she fervently hoped the switch to preparing Italian food wouldn't prove too difficult.

In Cairns Cesare collected the car and stowed their cases in the boot, wasting no time in driving out from the city towards the Kuranda Ranges. The car ascended the range swiftly, negotiating with controlled ease the innumerable winding bends as the road curved up towards the tablelands. Marisa viewed the surrounding terrain with interest, noting the different type of foliage. Here there were no cane paddocks to lend a fresh green aura to the landscape, and as they progressed further inland patches of red-brown sandy loam became evident in long stretches beside the asphalt of the road. Tall trees in the distance seemed to reach far up into the clear azure sky, and various peculiar-shaped anthills stood solid, like solemn sentinels, wherever she gazed. The wheels of the car set wooden bridge after wooden bridge rattling as they spanned numerous trickling creeks weaving their way down towards sea level. Farm buildings were beginning to appear among paddocks of waist-high green-leafed plants, which Cesare confirmed as tobacco. The air seemed clearer, more fresh somehow, and Marisa wondered just how high above sea-level they were.

The township of Mareeba appeared quite suddenly, its main street stretching long and wide, with huge trees spreading shade from the middle of the road. Modern buildings of concrete and sparkling glass mingled with old dwellings of weather-worn, sun-bleached wood. The car's speed checked slightly as they passed through, then increased rapidly once they traversed the creek on the outskirts of town. For almost twenty minutes they sped swiftly through tobacco country. The sun set the tarseal on the road shimmering, and the air was warm and dry as it breathed softly over the land surrounding them. The car slowed gently, and turned right, down a dirt road which sent clouds of red dust swirling from the rear wheels as they drove for a quarter of a mile before turning into a large yard.

Marisa looked about her with interest, noting the complex of farm buildings, the huge barn-like structures built of concrete blocks, connecting one after the other, and standing opposite, separated by a distance of fifty-odd feet or so, was a massive shed. The barns and shed were connected by a roof of corrugated iron, and under this stood two tractors, one utility truck, and a long trailer. Under a clump of mango trees three cars of various makes and ages were parked, one of which she recognised as Carlo's station-wagon. To the left, her gaze rested on a long barrack-like dwelling with at least eight doors leading off a verandah, that was obviously the workers' sleeping quarters.

Cesare slid out of the car, and Marisa hurriedly did likewise, hesitating silently as he took their cases from the boot, gazing at the solidly built, imposing brick home only a few yards away. As she mounted the steps behind his broad back, she felt the beginning of unease stir beneath her ribs.

'This is the kitchen,' Cesare indicated, with a sweep of his arm as she stepped into the large room, which was virtually a dining-room on one side, and a large ultra-modern kitchen on the other, separated by two room-dividers. The length of the dining-room table astounded her, and she mentally counted sixteen chairs neatly tucked beneath the gaily patterned vinyl-topped table. It must have been easily fifteen feet long and five feet wide. Help! she cried silently, let's hope these chairs are not all to be filled too soon.

Her incredulous eyes swept towards the kitchen, noting the gleaming electrical appliances and the abundance of built-in cupboards and formica-topped bench space. It looked adequate enough to cope with a restaurant clientele!

In silence she followed him into a lounge of sufficient proportions to accommodate two lounge-settees and several armchairs all upholstered in matching studded vinyl, a television, a stereo with speakers mounted high on the wall, and several coffee tables strategically placed between chairs, with ease. The floor held a highly polished sheen, no doubt due to several applications of polyurethane varnish, on which were scattered several sheepskin rugs.

From the lounge, she followed him through a wide archway into a long hall running at right angles from the kitchen, dining-room and lounge, and duly inspected a bathroom and four bedrooms, the last of which obviously was the master bedroom. Her eyes widened at the sight of the double bed with its brocade spread in peacock hues of blue and green. It was a large room, large enough to look spacious in spite of the long mirrored dressing-table and an equally long unit of drawers, capacious wardrobes, and an ornately carved linen chest.

She strove desperately to still the wave of panic surging through her veins as she clenched her hands tightly together behind her back. Cesare stood in the doorway, towering head and shoulders above her, quite at ease, and apparently unaware of the conflicting emotions whirling inside her brain.

'As you can see,' he drawled deeply, 'this is the main bedroom.' He stepped backwards, indicating that she should follow, and paused at the next doorway.

'You can use this room for a while,' he asserted steadily, and Marisa let go the breath she had unconsciously held over the past few seconds, and contrived to hide her relief.

'I'll be in the room on the other side of the bathroom,' he stated, lighting a cigarette and looking down at her through half-closed eyes. She was, he thought lazily, rather like a deprived child given its first sweet and ever so afraid the sugar coating might dissolve to reveal something bitter beneath. He expelled the smoke slowly, looking faintly quizzical.

'You have half an hour to change into your wedding finery and do to your face whatever it is you consider essential, before we leave for the Hall in Dimbulah.'

Before she could ask where she might iron her dress, he indicated a spare room at the other end of the hall. 'There's an ironing board in there.'

Twenty minutes later she was frowning into the mirror as she tried to do something with her hair. At last she managed to coax it into a style which looked presentable with her wedding attire, and she emerged from her room into the hall, and glimpsed Cesare waiting patiently in the lounge.

He regarded her enigmatically, and for an instant she had the sensation that time stood still, and she held her breath, conscious that her heart was pounding with—what?—Awareness? Attraction? Then the spell was broken at the sound of his voice.

'We'd better move,' he indicated, as she hovered in the archway, and shakily she followed him down the steps and slid into the car, feeling distinctly nervous at the prospect of being the centre of attention among so many strange people.

Why had he looked at her like that? The words echoed and re-echoed through her brain as the car sped swiftly westward.

The evening dusk was beginning to settle like a protective mantle over a slumbering earth when they reached the Hall, and at the large number of parked cars, Marisa felt the butterflies in her stomach turn somersaults. Her hand was taken and clasped firmly in Cesare's as they entered the brightly lit Hall.

Marisa glanced blindly around her, for there appeared to be at least a hundred people standing in scattered groups.

A cheer greeted them, which was both loud and tumultuous, and Marisa felt all eyes on her as Cesare led her down the centre of the hall to take their place at the head of the table.

'Speech! Speech! Speech!' roared all the men, and the women smiled indulgently and murmured among themselves.

Beside her, Cesare chuckled goodnaturedly, and began loudly in a voice they could all hear. '*Signori, signore, grazie*. I present to you, my wife, Marisa,' he paused to smile tenderly down at her, squeezing her hand gently as he glimpsed the nervous shaky smile on her pale face. 'It is very good to see you all, my friends, here this evening. And now,' he waved his hand towards the food-laden trestles, 'let's eat, and enjoy!'

There was a roar of approval as the guests cheered, '*Brava, brava!*' and seated themselves comfortably.

Champagne bottles were popped, glasses filled, and as Marisa sipped her champagne she shyly looked into the sea of nameless faces before her. The food was delicious, and under her husband's watchful eye she tried an assortment of food. The conversation all around her was entirely in Italian, and she felt at a loss to comprehend any of it. The speeches were also a mystery, and apart from the odd sentence directed to her in heavily accented English, she was left almost entirely in ignorance. Everyone seemed to be enjoying themselves immensely, if the cheerful rumble of noise was any indication.

At last everyone sat back from the tables, fully replete, and as the band struck the chords of a waltz, Cesare led her on to the floor and into his arms.

Oh dear, *why* did she have to feel so nervous of him? she tormented herself, as they completed a round of the floor. It wasn't as if she was *afraid* of him, not really, it was rather like being the fly in a spider's web waiting for the moment of truth!

Soon almost everyone was dancing, and Cesare bent his head down and spoke quietly into her ear.

'You're doing fine,' and she looked up, smiling hesitantly. Eventually the music stopped, and Cesare placed a casually possessive arm about her waist, leading her to the bridal table as the guests gathered together in an orderly queue to be formally introduced to Cesare's bride.

During the next hour she shook so many hands, and murmured 'pleased to meet you' so many times, her voice was husky and her head felt as if it didn't belong to her at all. The music drifted liltingly around them until the last guest had been formally greeted, and then Cesare pulled her gently into his arms for a dance.

Perhaps it was tiredness, or a feeling of unreality, but for one crazy moment she longed to rest her head against that broad chest only inches away. He's—nice, and—yes, *kind*, she thought sleepily, and I *like* him.

A large trestle laden with wedding presents intrigued her, and her heart softened with gratitude to all these people who had only met her for the first time tonight.

The music stopped, and she sipped some more champagne from the glass Cesare handed her, listening attentively to the group of men who had gathered around them, all speaking volubly about what, she knew not, but guessed was probably either tobacco or soccer, or both. Cesare kept an arm loosely about her waist, and she began to realise that the language barrier was going to present a problem for her with his friends, and she resolved to purchase a set of language records as soon as possible.

Carlo Rossini's wife, Rosa, must have felt sorry for her among all the men, for she came over and touched Marisa lightly on the arm.

'You come with me, Marisa,' she smiled. 'The men, you know, they talk soccer. You come with me.'

Cesare barely seemed to notice she had gone after he had given the briefest of nods to them both.

'You very lucky girl, to marry Cesare,' Rosa assured her as they wandered over to a group of women halfway down the hall. 'He's a very good man,' she endorsed, and then broke into Italian as she greeted the women, lapsing back into English within minutes. 'Sorry, Marisa, I forget.' She indicated each of the women in the group by name, and Marisa smiled shyly at them.

It was clear that they were genuinely curious about Cesare's quick marriage. Each of the women viewed her a trifle critically, she thought, and no doubt were wondering whether she would make Cesare a good wife, and prove herself suited to farm life. Her diminutive stature probably didn't compare very favourably with their buxom proportions fairly screaming with vigour and undaunting capability. Marisa felt doubly glad she had had the foresight to buy that recipe book. It would obviously be her constant companion for quite some time to come.

During the course of the next hour, various women drifted over to join them and speak with her, some young, some old, but all looking very energetic and capable. Marisa decided fiercely that she would keep pace with them, even if it killed her!

'Hi there!' a young female voice at her elbow caused her to start, and gather her scattered thoughts together.

'We're a bit awe-inspiring, en masse, aren't we?' the girl grinned wickedly, and Marisa smiled with relief that here was someone young, even younger, possibly, than she herself, *and* with a sense of humour.

'A bit, yes,' she acquiesced tentatively.

The other girl chuckled merrily. 'I won't give you away. My name's Tania Petricevic,' she gurgled with amusement. 'Cesare's kept you well hidden, or has it been one of those whirlwind romances?' she queried, quite unashamed of being inquisitive. 'Not that I blame you for snapping him up,' she continued pertly. 'To my knowledge, most doting mamas with marriageable daughters around here have been contriving to marry him off to their particular darling, for—oh, absolutely ages! He was quite the best catch on the going market!' She twinkled unrepentantly. 'Don't mind me, Marisa, I'm *glad* he chose you. We'll be friends, yes?'

Marisa couldn't help but smile. 'Yes,' she said gladly. 'Yes, I'd like that.'

Tania glowed with delight. 'I string for Cesare, sometimes, but I'll pay you a visit soon. After the Ingham tournament, probably. Oh-oh,' she cautioned softly, 'here's my fond mama, checking up on me.' She smiled, and beckoned her mother towards them.

Mrs Petricevic was slim, and bright-eyed, like her daughter, but her brow was creased into a worried frown as she reached them.

'Tania, where have you been? I could not see you anywhere!'

Tania smiled a ready warm smile, and said deprecatingly, 'Don't fuss, Mama, you'll get an ulcer. Marisa and I have been getting acquainted. I'm invited to visit, quite soon. Now, get that anxious look off your face, and *smile*, there's a dear.'

Mrs Petricevic's frown diminished slightly as she offered Marisa her hand.

'I'm pleased to meet you, Marisa,' she said in quaintly accented English. 'We all very happy that Cesare at last take a wife.' She nodded her head, and smiled again, for good measure.

Marisa pondered; the name—it wasn't Italian, was it?

'Dalmatian,' Tania informed her conspiratorially.

'You excuse, please?' Mrs Petricevic appeared anxious to return to the part of the hall from whence she had come.

Tania placed a friendly hand on Marisa's arm. ''Bye now.' Her eyebrows lifted expressively before she turned and followed her mother.

It was almost midnight when Cesare wandered over to collect Marisa from among the womenfolk, and she had to admit she was glad to see him.

'We'll get moving, it's quite late, and almost everyone is picking tomorrow,' he said quietly, taking her hand and moving towards the top of the hall, where, on a cacophonous chord from the band, he gave what Marisa took to be a speech of thanks to their guests.

The band began playing the strains of a final waltz, and Cesare slowly danced her the length of the hall, bidding all he passed on the way a cheerful goodnight. There were a few joking remarks flung at him by some of the older men, and at these, a deep genial chuckle escaped his throat. Marisa was sure the comments were cheeky, and she felt herself blushing beneath their frankly admiring glances.

At the car, Cesare held open the door and she slid in gratefully. She was overwhelmingly tired and already worrying what the next day would bring.

Cesare was quiet beside her as he drove homewards, and once inside, he looked down at her intently, his eyes, for one infinitesimal second, flaring sensually alive. A muscle at his jaw tightened momentarily, and then his expression softened as he gave her a gentle push.

'Go to bed, child. I'll wake you in the morning, at five, when the men come in for coffee. Breakfast is at seven-thirty, exactly. Goodnight.'

Marisa nodded forlornly, aware that there would be only a few hours sleep before she must rise and meet the trials of her first day.

'Goodnight,' she whispered tiredly, stifling a yawn, as she went ahead of him to her room. Bed had never looked so good, and she quickly undressed and slipped between the cool crisp sheets.

CHAPTER SEVEN

THE sound of her name being called, accompanied by a knock on her door, roused Marisa into wakefulness, and she glanced at her watch in disbelief, sure that she had only just gone to sleep. With a silent groan she saw that it was a quarter to five, and obviously time to rise and shine. She slipped into her brunch-coat and answered that she was awake.

When she reached the kitchen five minutes later, Cesare was already there, looking intensely fit and muscular in beige denim working shorts and shirt. He opened numerous cupboards and quickly indicated where crockery and utensils were to be found, then took a slip of folded paper from beneath the coffee percolator.

'Rosa has listed the times of meals and smokos, also what you should cook for breakfast. There's a laundry outside, there,' he indicated, and she obediently looked out at the building a few yards from the back door. 'Rosa will be over after breakfast, so any questions you have, you can ask her, okay?' He was very brisk and impersonal, gone were the gentle overtones of the past few days. It was down to earth with a bang, Marisa mused thoughtfully.

With a matching briskness, she set about providing coffee and biscuits for the men, and no sooner had she poured the coffee into cups than she heard the thud of footsteps on the steps, and the screen-door opened to admit four men of various ages.

Marisa glanced at them, smiling shyly as Cesare introduced them in order of appearance. The men eyed her a little dubiously, or so she thought, and with a hesitant 'excuse me' she slipped out of the kitchen.

Her suitcases which Carlo had brought up from the cottage were neatly stacked in the wardrobe of the master bedroom, and she lost no time unpacking them. Luckily very little needed ironing, and in any case, she could tackle it later. Rather timidly she entered Cesare's room and made his bed. She felt slightly guilty at invading his wardrobe as she put things away, and completed the task as quickly as the bounds of tidiness would allow.

In the kitchen she boiled the jug and made herself a cup of instant coffee, preferring a milder brew at that hour of the morning, and sat down at a table with Rosa's fateful list. It was very concisely written in badly spelt English, and by the time Marisa had finished deciphering it she was so nervous that she wouldn't be able to cope, she felt like weeping. After a few minutes' self-pity, she reflected on those critical looks of the previous evening and stood to her feet, determined to match up to their standard.

A quick reconnoitre of all the cupboards and drawers in the kitchen gave her some idea of where everything was kept. The refrigerator was well stocked, and the deep-freeze was almost full with meat and poultry of every description.

Quickly and carefully she worked, an anxious frown creasing her brow as the sound of a distant tractor drew nearer.

Cesare came into the house a few seconds ahead of the men, and cast a cursory glance over the table, then swept his gaze to Marisa's slight figure hovering in the kitchen undecided whether to eat with them or wait until later. One glance at Cesare's face was sufficient, and she hurriedly took her place at the table.

Marisa was amazed at the speed with which the men ate their food. Within ten minutes their plates were bare, their coffee drained, and they were clattering down the steps into the yard. Cesare lingered only long enough to inform her that lunch must be ready at twelve, *pronto*.

Phew! She cleared the table, washed and dried dishes, then swept the kitchen and dining-room floor. One down, and two meals to go. She was on the point of carrying some clothes out to the laundry when Rosa appeared.

'Good morning, Marisa. How are you?' She smiled at Marisa in a cheerful friendly fashion, her dark hair pulled back into a nondescript bun at the nape of her neck, and an apron tied at her waist. She was a tall woman of buxom proportions, and Marisa idly put her age at around mid-thirties.

'Hello, Rosa. I'm fine, thank you,' she welcomed, sincerely glad to see her, for since reading that list she realised she needed Rosa's assistance quite badly.

'I come to help you. You know, show you Italian way of cooking,' she began, following Marisa into the dining-room.

'We sit here, yes?' Rosa indicated the table and sat down in one of the chairs. 'You get pencil and paper. My English writing, it not too good,' she shook her head in despair.

'I do appreciate your help, Rosa,' Marisa began. 'I've bought an Italian recipe book. Will that help?'

Rosa nodded enthusiastically, and Marisa collected a notebook and pen, the recipe book, and together they began to work out an outline of meals. Marisa's pen flew as she wrote down hint after hint, and marked recipes which Rosa selected as suitable. After an hour, her head was reeling, and she was relieved when Rosa suggested they view the complex of farm buildings together.

'I come again tomorrow morning, and we carry on, yes?' Rosa queried, and Marisa accepted the offer gladly.

They went outside into the yard, and as they walked, Marisa took note of all the chickens barely six weeks old that must be fed, the fifty-odd fowls and few roosters. There was a separate pen with ducks and numerous ducklings, and yet another pen with six turkeys. All for Marisa to look after, Rosa informed her. Help! There was a faithful black and white spaniel with long silky black ears and soulful eyes named Pepe, who was Cesare's, and she needed no second bidding to choose a little kitten from Rosa's feline litter of four. They continued walking, and Rosa indicated a neatly fenced-off garden planted in row upon row of vegetables of almost every description. Marisa began to see why no self-respecting housekeeper would stay very long. All this—it was a labour of love, by a woman, for her man!

They had come almost full circle, and beneath the long verandah between the barns and the bulking shed Rosa outlined briefly the method of curing tobacco. Eight women were standing beside wooden stands rapidly stringing green tobacco leaves on to sticks approximately three feet in length, and Rosa explained that as they were paid by the stick, the higher the number of sticks strung, the higher the pay.

The sound of a tractor grew closer, and within minutes it roared to a halt under the far end of the verandah. Marisa saw Cesare behind the wheel and watched with fascination as he leapt to the ground and effortlessly lifted large bundles of tobacco leaves rolled together with sacking down from the trailer on to trestles. She couldn't help a surge of pride that he was her husband, even though the mere thought disturbed her more than she wanted to admit. And that, she thought with a sudden flash of humour, was just about as mixed-up as you could get!

With a sketchy wave in their direction, Cesare swung himself up on to the tractor, backed it out, and sent it roaring out into the paddock.

Rosa shook her hear regretfully as Marisa asked if she would like to come back for coffee.

'Thank you, but no. If there's anything you want to know, you come over to my house, please? Otherwise, I see you tomorrow morning.' She almost scurried to her house, and with a quick glance at her watch Marisa hastily made for hers, realising she had only an hour and a half to prepare lunch.

The next hour was a busy one, for she was extremely conscious of the time element, but finally with a sigh of satisfaction she stood waiting for the men to arrive.

As before, they came from the paddock, washed up outside, and filed in to sit down and eat without any waste of time. Cesare collected a carafe of red wine from the fridge and put it on the table beside the jug of iced water. After the men left, he poured another glass of wine and leaning well back in his chair surveyed her as she cleared the table and sorted dishes into the sink.

'Who's doing smoko this afternoon?' he queried. 'You, or Rosa?'

Marisa turned off the taps, and answered that she was.

'The tractor will be in about three, I'll come and collect it.' He stood up and tucked his chair under the table. 'Carlo and I are going into Dimbulah to the Hall to pick up those boxes of wedding presents. You'd better decide where you want them by the time we get back. *Ciao.*' He moved quickly from the house to the verandah, and from the kitchen window she saw him ease the ute down the drive with Carlo following closely behind in the station-wagon.

Wedding presents! She'd forgotten all about them. The spare bedroom would be best, she thought quickly, for they could be stacked there until after dinner when she would have a chance to begin unpacking and sorting them out. It was something to look forward to, and she felt a thrill of anticipation at unwrapping so many gifts. The house was lovely enough now, and there appeared to be plenty of saucepans, crockery and utensils. There was nothing really *needed.*

She had just placed a cake in the oven and was buttering bread when Cesare and Carlo returned. They made several trips back and forth from the station-wagon and ute with armloads of differently assorted boxes, which at her direction were placed in the spare room.

The light fruit cake was a success and it smelt delicious as it lay on the cooling rack. There were only the sandwiches to finish, and at three on the dot she had the tea made. The food reposed neatly in its napkin-lined wicker basket, and she had cleared the kitchen ready for another onslaught.

As good as his word, Cesare entered the kitchen a few minutes after three to collect the basket and tea-kettle.

'Dinner at six-fifteen sharp, Marisa.' The instruction was curtly delivered, and she barely had time to assent before he left, the screen-door banging behind him.

Not a word of praise or thanks, she thought dejectedly. Oh well, she consoled herself, at least she hadn't made any ghastly mistakes, so far. *So far!* The most important meal of the day was still to come!

Standing at the bench with recipe book to her right and her copious notes to the left, she decided on an attempt at spaghetti for dinner, with roast chicken, roast potatoes and a green vegetable to follow. Rosa had stressed that only one green vegetable accompanied the evening meat dish, whether it be silverbeet, cabbage, beans, or a salad.

An hour later Marisa gave a contented sigh that dinner was well on the way. Now perhaps she might have a chance to explore the laundry. Much to her delight the washing machine was fully automatic. The work might be hard and the hours long, but at least there seemed to be every labour-saving device to help, she mused thankfully.

While the washing took care of itself she decided to have a cup of coffee and a well earned sit-down for five minutes, wondering idly as she did so how Tony was enjoying his first day at college.

Thanks to Rosa and the recipe book, dinner was a success. Her husband leaned forward in the midst of eating his spaghetti and imparted his approval by saying that her spaghetti was very good. The men thought so, too, for they nodded their heads in agreement. Marisa's spirits soared and she smiled warmly at them all, grateful that her careful effort had not gone unnoticed.

The men conversed in their own language, so like a dutiful wife she bent her head and ate her food in silence, trying to make up her mind whether she was hurt or relieved that Cesare made no further attempt to speak to her during the meal.

Soon it was dishes again, stacks of them! Marisa shuddered to think what it would be like when there were seven or eight men in a few more weeks. She applied herself to the task diligently, and by seven-thirty the kitchen and dining-room were clean and tidy again.

Cesare appeared in the doorway of the spare bedroom a while later, a slight smile on his face at the picture she made sitting on the floor surrounded by boxes and wrapping paper.

'There's quite a collection there,' he stated, observing the happy flush on her cheeks and the sparkle in her eyes.

'Yes, there is, isn't there?' she breathed with excitement and glanced up at him. 'There're some really beautiful things, do you want to see them all?'

He shook his head, drawing a cigarette from its pack and lighting it. 'No, you sort them out and find a home for them.' He crouched down beside her to examine some crystal sherry glasses, and she felt her stomach turn over. Why, *why* did she have to feel so attracted to him? Why not? her conscience prodded her.

'You'll have quite a job ahead of you getting all these washed and put away.' He stood up, towering over her. 'I'll be in the bulking shed with Carlo for a couple of hours yet, we have a barn to take out. Don't work at it too late.'

Reaching the decision to deal with the glasses and crockery first, Marisa carried them out to the kitchen in relays and proceeded to wash and dry them all carefully. Finding space for them was not difficult, for there were plenty of cupboards. There were a few pairs of blankets and a quantity of linen and towels, and these she stored away in the large carved chest in the master-bedroom.

She carefully placed the cards from the presents in the top drawer of her dressing-table, and with a glance at her watch decided to get ready for bed. The day had been a demanding one and she was suddenly overwhelmingly tired.

The next day began as it had yesterday, with Cesare knocking on her door at a quarter to five. This time however, she had the beds made, the poultry fed and the garden watered before breakfast and when Rosa came after breakfast they spent a further hour engrossed with the recipe book as Marisa made copious notes.

The poultry in the deep-freeze was still plentiful, but guided by Rosa's advice on the necessity to kill and freeze the poultry when the chickens were at their plumpest and tenderest, she broached the subject with Cesare and received the shock of her life when he made it obvious that she must catch, kill and clean all the poultry she needed.

She just looked at him, aghast. 'Cesare! I couldn't possibly do that!' she exclaimed, horrified. 'It's cruel! I mean, I know they have to be killed, and—and——' but he interrupted her very firmly, with an authoritative gleam in those dark eyes.

'No, Marisa. I'm in the paddock most of the time. You must do it yourself. Ask Rosa, she'll show you how.'

The subject was closed, and with a sinking heart she knew he would not relent.

It was after lunch the next day when she slipped

over to Rosa's house for the first time, determined to get the poultry over and done with.

Rosa welcomed her enthusiastically and invited her inside, casting aside her apron and pulling out a chair.

'You have problem, yes?' she queried. 'I can help?'

Marisa nodded ruefully, and mentioned her dilemma.

'Ah, *si, si.* Always you must kill them at four, perhaps five months old. That way they plump and tender and take not too long for cooking. You never kill chicken before? No?' she queried incredulously, obviously staggered at this omission in Marisa's domestic education.

'No,' Marisa grinned a trifle sheepishly. 'Cesare says I must, so I have to learn and he said you would show me.'

Rosa nodded, and rose to her feet briskly. 'You come with me, we do it now.'

Marisa followed her reluctantly to the chicken-pen, and watched with awe as Rosa opened the door and stepped inside. In two seconds flat she caught up a bird in her hand and brought it close to the fence to demonstrate the method necessary to pull and twist the wretched bird's neck. Marisa turned pale, feeling quite ill, and fairly shook when Rosa bade her enter the pen to catch one and do likewise.

She soon realised that it was not as easy as it looked, and after ten minutes stopped bothering to select which bird she would catch. It was enough if she could catch one, *any* one, never mind *which* one! Finally she grabbed one by the wing, holding the wildly fluttering, madly squawking *thing* as she tried to grip its neck. She pulled and twisted, all to no avail until finally, with tears pouring her cheeks, she at last broke its neck.

'*Brava, brava!*' The droll sound of Cesare's voice unnerved her completely.

Marisa clutched at the dead fowl and could cheerfully have flung the wretched bird at him! She watched furiously as he pushed his rather crumpled broad-brimmed straw hat on to the back of his head, a smile twitching at the corner of his mouth. He thought it was funny! Ohhh! Men!

Cesare indicated his approval, his eyes gleaming rather wickedly as he slid his hat forward and strode round the side of the pen towards the verandah.

Marisa fumed inwardly, vowing that one day, *one day*, just you *wait*, Cesare Gianelli!

Rosa's voice brought her attention back to the problem at hand. 'Come, Marisa, we hang the birds under the tree for a little while. The water, it will boil soon, then I show you how to pluck and clean them.'

Feeling considerably shaken, Marisa nodded absently, following Rosa back across the yard. The large pail on the stove was indeed nearly boiling, and Rosa quickly filled a bucket and spread newspaper over the bench. The fowls were fetched and with a speed that amazed her, Rosa stripped them of their feathers and began to instruct Marisa on the best method of disembowelling them.

Marisa felt ill, sure that if she was ever to do it successfully in the future, she would have to wear rubber gloves. Ugghh!

Back in her own kitchen a short while later she unwrapped the offending birds from the newspaper, pushed them into plastic bags and slid them quickly in the deep-freeze. So much for that! Rosa had intimated that ducks were much worse, and as for turkeys——! Her eyes had rolled heavenwards. Marisa silently cursed her unlucky stars and prayed God help her!

After dinner she wrote a long newsy letter to Tony, full of snippets about farm life and their proposed trip to Ingham for the soccer tournament. She re-read the letter and addressed an envelope, noting wearily that it was past ten o'clock. Another day awaited her tomorrow, and no doubt would prove as instructive as today had been. Just so long as she didn't have to tackle any more poultry. At least, not yet awhile, she prayed fervently as she switched off her light.

CHAPTER EIGHT

It seemed almost an anti-climax as they drove away from the farm after lunch on Friday, en route for Ingham. Four days with no cooking, no chores, no nuthin'. Marisa felt like tossing her hat over the moon!

The car purred along like a leashed tiger beneath Cesare's competent touch, and Marisa leaned well back, enjoying the well-sprung upholstery.

'We have to stop at the Graham Hotel for a while to sort out transport,' he said briskly as he lit a cigarette and then pocketed the packet and matches. He blew the smoke out the window and cast a quick glance in her direction. 'We may have to give one of the players a lift down, not everyone is taking their car.'

Marisa turned to meet those dark eyes and managed a smile. 'Are there many going down, besides the players, I mean?' she asked, and saw that they weren't far from the outskirts of Mareeba.

'Quite a few, I imagine. We have a number of supporters, and most of the committee members will go down. I believe the hotel we're booked into is almost completely taken over by Mareeba players and supporters.' He slowed down as they approached the Graham Hotel and swung the big car into the kerb.

'I shouldn't be long,' he said brusquely, as he slid out from behind the wheel and slammed the door behind him.

She sat wondering idly how long it would take to get to Ingham, who, if anyone, they would take down with them, and lastly, but certainly not least, whether or not there would be single beds in their room at the hotel. If there weren't—well, it didn't bear thinking about.

It was all of half an hour before Cesare emerged from the hotel with a slimmer, shorter, younger man at his side. They came over to the car and Cesare slung the canvas holdall into the boot before tipping his seat forward to allow their passenger to get into the back seat.

'Alan, my wife, Marisa. Alan Parker, our only non-Italian player,' he indicated to Marisa as he turned on the ignition and set the car moving backwards on to the street.

Marisa smiled as she turned in her seat, and liked what she saw. Alan was perhaps twenty-three or twenty-four, and he looked fresh and uncomplicated, and not difficult to converse with.

'It's good of you not to mind giving me a lift,' he grinned at her. 'As you're so newly married, I wouldn't blame Cesare for wanting to keep you to himself,' he chuckled and closed one eye in a wicked wink. She blushed and decided no reply to that remark was needed.

'I was only kidding—don't, for heaven's sake, take me seriously,' he hastened to amend, still grinning cheekily as he took cigarettes and matches from his pocket and offered them to Cesare, who took one with muttered thanks.

Marisa decided to try to put the conversation on to a less personal footing, and began matter-of-factly:

'Do you live in Mareeba permanently, Alan?'

'Yes, born and bred. Dad operates the Esso garage, and I help out.' He leaned forward to catch the lighted match Cesare offered over his shoulder.

'What do you think of the place?' he queried as he sat back in the rear of the car.

'I like it,' she replied at once. 'The town is quite a bit larger than I expected, and there seem to be a great number of outlying farms.'

Alan nodded as the car sped on to the main highway, en route to Cairns. 'Yes, it's the largest tobacco-growing area in the whole of Australia. We also have a terrific rodeo here, you've missed it this year, but it's quite a show. They have a tobacco queen, a festival, and a parade—we do ourselves proud. This town has really gone ahead over the last few years. The population is well sprinkled with Italians, Yugoslavs, Sicilians, Albanians. They outnumber us dinky-die Aussies easily four to one,' he laughed companionably.

'I believe the whole of Ingham is fully booked out, hotel-wise, Cesare,' he commented.

'Yes, I believe so,' Cesare answered with a slight smile. 'I think our crowd have taken over one hotel, and I shouldn't be surprised if there's not a spare bed anywhere in Ingham.'

'Are we shooting straight through, or making the usual customary stops on the way?' Alan queried.

Cesare laughed, and replied with amusement, 'Oh, I daresay we'll find the need to down a few beers on the way—Cairns first, of course.'

'Jolly good, although I guess Fred will see to it we have only one glass at each. Worse than a hawk, that man,' he enlightened Marisa.

For the remainder of the long drive, punctuated as anticipated with several halts for liquid refreshments of alcoholic variety, they chatted easily and companionably. As they approached the outskirts of yet another township an enveloping blanket of darkness had settled around them, plunging the countryside into obscurity. Marisa's interest quickened as Cesare indicated the twinkling lights visible in the distance and announced that they had almost reached their destination.

Much to her relief, their hotel room held two single beds, and at Cesare's injunction to leave the unpacking until after they'd eaten, she quickly ran a comb through her hair and followed him from the room.

In a nearby café she viewed her plate of chicken and salad with relish, not realising until then just how hungry she was. Apart from a brief enquiry to ascertain her preference for tea or coffee Cesare immersed himself in a debate with four players at an adjoining table.

As they strolled along the pavement towards their hotel Marisa drew a startled breath as Cesare caught her hand and held it imprisoned within his. Her fingers moved slightly, convulsively, of their own volition within his grasp as she fought valiantly to calm the nervous thudding of her heart. Rather absently his thumb moved across the veins at her wrist in what presumably was meant to be a soothing gesture, and Marisa suppressed an involuntary shiver at the sheer physical magnetism his action aroused. She felt frightened and a little bewildered as he drew her into the bright jovial noisiness of the hotel beer-garden and fetched drinks for them both from the bar. The tight knot of nerves in the region of her stomach relaxed somewhat after her second Cinzano, and it was with surprise she saw the hotel doors begin to close.

The team manager, Alfredo—Fred—Bombardi, shooed the players upstairs to their rooms, adamant in spite of their protests that it was early. Tomorrow the team must play soccer, and that was sacrosanct.

Marisa divested the contents of their two cases into drawers, and hung what was necessary in the wardrobe, all the time feeling dreadfully aware of Cesare's presence in the room. It was all she could do not to breathe an audible sigh of relief when he elected to have a shower and disappeared out into the hallway. Shakily she caught up her nightgown and brunch-coat and set out down the hall in search of the women's bathroom facilities, mentally admonishing herself to regain her composure as she leisurely showered, revelling in the exquisitely perfumed talc she sprinkled liberally all over her glowing body. It was ridiculous to be so afraid of him. But was it fear of him, or the awareness he aroused within her that was responsible for this tremulous longing for something more tangible? Thoroughly cross with herself by now, and vexed by her inexperience, she returned to their room with her clothes on her arm, and felt the blush creep over her cheeks at the sight of Cesare sitting in bed calmly smoking as he read the local newspaper.

His dark eyes gleamed with amusement at her obvious discomfort and her indecision whether to be brave in discarding her brunch-coat while the light was still on.

'I have seen the female form attired in less,' he commented teasingly as she hovered hesitantly. 'My existence has been far from monkish, but I assure you I shan't leap out of bed and seduce you at the sight of a decorative lacy frill or two.'

She felt her cheeks flame, and choked back an indignant retort.

'I didn't for one moment think you would,' she managed at last. 'I'm not a child,' she finished with dignity, turning back the covers on her bed.

'In years, perhaps not,' he agreed quietly. 'If you were other than the young innocent I know you to be, you would not sleep in that bed alone, *carina*.' He stubbed out his cigarette in the ashtray on the table between their beds and regarded her with something akin to indulgence. 'Stop trembling and get into bed, I can reach the light switch from here. Goodnight.'

Marisa managed a strangled 'goodnight' in return, and quickly discarded her brunch-coat, slipping beneath the sheets hastily as he flicked the switch and plunged the room into darkness.

It was wonderful not to have to cook breakfast, merely to be able to sit down and have a meal brought to her. Feeling like this after only five days of being a housewife! It seemed to taste better somehow, she mused, tucking into poached eggs on toast.

The Mareeba team was playing the second game of the day, timed for commencement at two o'clock, but naturally everyone intended viewing the morning match to watch and criticise, to take note of the various players' techniques. It was the first time Marisa had watched soccer, and she had to admit there was a great deal of skill involved. It was intensely interesting, for these men seemed to put all they had into playing. This was no friendly-Sunday-afternoon game, they were deadly earnest and all out to win. Cesare was by her side, but in spirit he was out there on the field, as indeed it appeared were most of the men. They shouted, they swore, they waved their arms with such abandon that Marisa had to watch for her safety on numerous occasions. The advice they shouted to individual players from time to time, in fact nearly *all* of the time, was both concise and pithy. For Marisa, who had rarely been to any type of football game, this was a revelation.

Lunch was partaken of at a café in town, and although the match was not due to start for a further hour, the Mareeba players drove to the sports field, changed, massaged liniment into thigh and calf muscles, did physical jerks, and earnestly discussed their tactics.

By the time the match began, Marisa had absorbed much of the spectators' enthusiasm and felt excitement grip sharply as the game progressed. Cesare possessed a dynamic action and his skill at the game was evident. Marisa found herself cheering along with everyone else when Mareeba triumphed to win by two goals over their opponents.

An hour later she found herself ensconced in a chair surrounded by men with the company of two of the players' wives—unfortunately unable to speak any English—utterly lost amidst a sea of gesticulating, loudly debating, mad Italians! It was almost dark before someone remembered they hadn't eaten, and the hotel lounge was vacated in favour of a nearby café.

Fred Bombardi proved an insistent mentor and shepherded them all back to their hotel by closing time.

Marisa turned the covers from her bed and slipped off her brunch-coat with apparent unconcern, although she doubted Cesare was fooled as he regarded her lazily over the top of his book. His brief 'goodnight' held hidden laughter, and she wished she had the bravado to throw her pillow at him as she was sorely tempted to do. She perceived from the lambent smouldering of those dark eyes that that *would* be asking for trouble!

Sunday was a repetition of Saturday with the exception that the match went into extra time. The whole atmosphere was even more tension-charged than it had been before, and after what seemed to be an interminable battle, Mareeba scored the winning goal.

To celebrate, Fred Bombardi condescended to allow the players to join in the dancing in their hotel lounge that evening. Marisa found herself sitting at a table among all men, with Cesare at her left and Alan on her right. Cesare seemed completely oblivious to her, and the others were all talking in voluble Italian, so it seemed inevitable that she and Alan should lapse into conversation.

'We're right through to the final, now,' Alan began, leaning slightly towards her, and Marisa turned a little, and smiled.

'Yes, it's fantastic,' she agreed, sipping her shandy. 'Do you think you have a show of winning tomorrow?'

'Well, that's in the lap of the gods. Innisfail is a very good team, and their goalkeeper is A-1. He seems to attract the ball into his hands like a magnet. It'll be difficult to score, but we can only play as hard as we can and hope for the best. I say, you must be a bit lost this trip, neither Elsa nor Tina speak any English.' He blew smoke out over his shoulder and stubbed his cigarette in the ashtray. 'You'll have to learn the lingo, Marisa, or you're in for a lonely time.'

'I intend to, just as soon as I find the time and the opportunity,' she enlightened him with a grin. 'Up until now I've managed with a great deal of sign language and an attempt at pidgin English, which is awful, really, for I suppose they learn from us, too, and the least we should do is to speak correctly. Cesare,' she ventured, 'has barely an accent at all.'

Alan poured himself another beer from the bottle on the table. 'Ah, yes, but then he was well educated in Italy before he came out here, and he has made the effort to study the language and correct diction. It makes a difference,' he went on to elaborate. 'Don't get me wrong, I'm not knocking immigrants at all, but in the main, the Italians, Yugoslavs, Spanish—you name them—they come into a community where there are large numbers of their fellow-countrymen, and they just sit back and make little effort to learn a new language. Why should they? There's always someone in the hotel, shop, or wherever, who will understand them. You can't wholly blame them, I suppose—our language is one of the most difficult to learn, so they say, as a secondary language, that is.'

'I guess you're right,' she contemplated speculatively, finding it difficult to converse to the accompaniment of the noisily enthusiastic band.

'I hate to agree,' he said cheekily, 'but I know I am. Besides, they view us with a certain amount of disdain. Their ancestors go back in time to the great Roman Empire, whereas ours, more recently anyway, were banished from the motherland to the Commonwealth convict continent!'

Marisa laughed reproachfully, 'Oh, Alan, that's scarcely a true comparison!'

He shrugged. 'Maybe not, but what the hell, we're not going to get embroiled in a political discussion, ancient though it may be. Come on, that music's developing a real beat. Hey, Cesare,' he leaned across behind her back and touched Cesare's shoulder. 'Do you mind if I dance with Marisa?'

Cesare inclined his head, waved an arm for them to go ahead, then returned his attention to the discussion he had been so deeply engrossed in.

'Come on, Marisa, you *do* dance, twist, whatever?' Alan encouraged as she murmured, 'After a fashion,' indistinctly.

'We'll show 'em!' He pulled up and led her on to the dance floor.

Well, he was no amateur at the twist, that was for sure, Marisa perceived, as he gyrated on the floor with expertise. She was hard put to follow him, and contented herself with a fairly inhibited display. He grinned, indicating that she should try to follow his movements, and she laughed and shook her head. He was impossible!

The music went on and on, couples drifted on and off the floor, and it was as she was trying to keep up with Alan to a particularly wild beat that she chanced to catch Cesare's eye. If looks could kill, she would have died on the spot. The icy anger evident in those dark eyes, before he looked away, chilled her to her very bones, and she cursed herself for not realising that he would not appreciate her dancing with Alan for as long as she had. He was not a man to be treated lightly, and she trembled that he might demand retribution. Her limbs seemed suddenly like jelly, and she indicated to Alan that she wished to return to their table. He shrugged, then followed her as she threaded her way through the dancing couples.

She sat down shakily, answering Alan monosyllabically, sitting in strained silence, aware that Cesare had not so much as given her a glance since she had returned to his side.

Shortly afterwards Fred Bombardi indicated that the players should retire for the evening as the final, and most important, game was the following day.

She preceded Cesare into their room and gathered her things in preparation for a shower, quickly slipping into the hallway en route to the bathroom. He made no attempt to stop her and she took as long as she dared before returning, fear and uncertainty causing havoc with her nerves.

Only the wall-light was glowing when she opened the door, and she saw at once his powerful frame in front of the window as he looked through the heavy net curtain down on to the street below. With shaking fingers she hung her dress in the wardrobe and spread her towel over the back of the chair. As she straightened and turned round, he was standing only inches away, towering over her, his eyes leaping with barely concealed fury. Steel-like arms pulled her close, and she gasped out loud, too frightened to struggle.

Her eyes were large dark pools as she looked up at him, startled almost out of her mind at the savage intensity of his expression. Her lips parted slightly to implore with him, but his head descended, his lips meeting hers with slow, almost cruel deliberation. There was no escape from the relentless pressure of that punishing mouth as his lips moved to the golden skin at the hollow of her throat. He eased the flimsy nylon strap of her nightgown down over her shoulder as his lips trailed flame across delicate hollows to the soft budding swell beneath. He lifted his head slowly, his eyes sensually alive as they roved intimately over the contours of her face, then his mouth fastened on hers and his hands caressed her with frightening expertise.

A choking sob stuck in her throat, and at last he lifted his head. Humiliated and very near to tears, she looked up at him, almost unable to see his face through a watery mist as the tears welled and spilled over, running down in twin rivulets to drip from her chin. Dear God, she silently begged, please, not in anger. *Please*, she implored him, her lips trembling as she sought to still her shaking limbs, her eyes mesmerised by his.

With fingers that were surprisingly gentle he smoothed the tears from her face, lightly touching her bruised lips with a stray finger.

'You are my wife, Marisa,' he said quietly. 'Never arouse my anger by flirting with another man, as you did tonight. I can assure you,' his voice hardened, 'you will have cause to regret it.'

Perhaps there was reproach in her expression at this, for in all sincerity she had not been aware that she had been flirting. She had laughed at Alan, with him even, and had talked with him, but surely it couldn't be considered flirting?

'I am Italian,' he offered quietly by way of explanation, 'and you are my wife. To dance as you did tonight with someone other then myself is unacceptable.'

He turned away, suddenly impatient. 'Go to bed. It is late. Goodnight.'

Shakily Marisa moved to her bed, slipping in between the sheets as he switched off the light. She heard his bed creak, and she lay awake, trembling, for a long while before finally drifting into an uneasy sleep, from which she awakened early with a throbbing headache. After lying there for ages in the semi-darkness of the room, she elected to have a hot shower in the hope that it might ease her a little, and slipped quietly from her bed.

Cesare appeared to be sleeping soundly, and for a fleeting moment she viewed his relaxed features. As her gaze came to rest at his mouth, she shivered involuntarily, the memory of those lips on hers still very vivid in her mind. Cautiously she turned away to collect her brunch-coat from the end of her bed, slipping her arms inside the sleeves and fumbling with the buttons.

'You're up early—can't you sleep?'

At the sound of his voice she jumped with fright, and ran a shaky hand through her hair.

'Yes—no—I—I have a headache, that's all,' she mumbled inarticulately, unable to face him.

'Is it bad?' His voice held a note of concern as she gathered her towel and a selection of fresh underwear.

Marisa managed a non-committal reply and became panic-stricken as his bed creaked. The towel slipped from her fingers as she sought to control her shaking limbs. Seconds later she felt his hands on her shoulders as he turned her back to face him, and her chin was taken firmly and lifted upwards so that she had to look at him or close her eyes.

He would have had to be very hard-hearted not to be moved by the dark smudges beneath eyes that were clouded with pain, and he swore softly before gathering her into his arms. He held her against him, lightly smoothing her tumbled hair with gentle fingers until her ragged breathing gradually calmed. She felt the light fleeting touch of his lips on her forehead.

'I'll ring for coffee and toast, and ask for some codeine,' he said quietly, releasing her, and turned to the phone on the table beside the bed.

Within a short while there was a knock at their door, and a maid delivered a tray which Cesare took and set down on the table. There was toast and marmalade, a large pot of coffee, two cups and saucers, and a small packet of tablets.

When Cesare left for the dining-room over an hour later, her headache had begun to improve slightly and while he was away she went for a shower. She had assured him she couldn't face anything else to eat, and that was true enough. The hot needle-spray of the shower revived her and she was beginning to feel back in the world of the living by the time he returned.

He cast her a penetrating look as he closed the door behind him.

'How is it?' he queried as he took cigarettes and matches from his pocket. Marisa wondered idly how many he smoked a day—more than a packet, easily.

'Quite a bit better, thank you,' she replied politely as he struck a match and put it to the cigarette in his mouth. He expelled the smoke slowly as he stood looking down at her.

'We play in the final this afternoon. I suggest you stay here and rest until lunch-time.'

'Would you mind?' she enquired tentatively, unaccountably relieved when he shook his head.

'Not in the least. I'll have some magazines sent up, and collect you at midday for lunch.'

The prospect of a lazy morning was pleasant, and when Cesare left shortly after nine she went out on to the terrace with some magazines and sat back in the deck-chair with enjoyment. The headache had eased to a mere niggle, and she knew if she took two more codeine in another hour it would disappear altogether.

Marisa resolved to put out of her mind as much as possible the events of the previous evening. There seemed little point in dwelling on it, for Cesare obviously had no intention of apologising. She doubted he had ever apologised for his actions to any woman!

She was drowsing pleasantly beneath the warmth of the sun when the door from their room on to the terrace opened, and Cesare stood and surveyed her tolerantly for several seconds, musing that it was a shame to disturb her.

'Wake up, lazy-bones,' he commanded softly from behind her chair, and gently tugged at her hair.

She opened her eyes lethargically, unable to believe the time had gone so quickly. 'Is it lunch-time already?'

He nodded, smiling broadly as she made no effort to rise.

'On your feet, child, you have ten minutes before we leave for the café.'

Hastily she scrambled up from the chair and gathered the magazines together. She did feel hungry, and mercifully her head was completely clear.

'You look much better,' he observed, submitting her to a searching appraisal, and she nodded, managing to meet those dark inscrutable eyes.

'I feel fine now, my head belongs to me again.'

'Good,' he commented crisply, and turned away to collect his soccer gear together.

Marisa quickly delved into her make-up case and began applying moisturiser, powder and lipstick. Her hair she simply caught at each side of her face with slides, and slipped her bare feet into cork-heeled sandals. There, that should do, she viewed herself critically in the mirror.

The final match was due to begin at two o'clock, and from the start the pace was rigorous. The play was rough and hard, for each team was out to win, and several players were warned by the referee about their near infringement of the rules. It was an exciting game to watch, and at half-time the score was equal with one goal apiece. The second half was even more harsh than the first, and more than once Marisa felt alarm. Someone was bound to get hurt sooner or later.

It was shortly afterwards that it happened. Cesare and his opponent were battling for the ball with their feet, each striving to get it free, when Cesare's ankle received a resounding kick. Heart in mouth, Marisa watched breathlessly as he was helped off the field and examined by two first-aid attendants. She stood on the fringe of the group surrounding him, anxiously wishing someone would explain in English the extent of Cesare's injuries.

It seemed from his expressive mutterings Cesare refused to sit down and had every intention of watching the remainder of the game.

With a shaking head and several mutterings of his own, one of the first-aid attendants helped Cesare to his feet, and Marisa managed to inch her way through several spectators to stand at his side.

'Is—his ankle broken?' she enquired tentatively.

The man nodded, shrugging his shoulders in exasperation. 'He should go now to the hospital and have an X-ray. But will he go? No! He insists on staying until the end of the game!' He threw his hands up into the air, and Marisa turned towards Cesare with a worried frown.

'Cesare, don't you think you should? It's foolish not to go,' she pleaded with him, but he waved a negligent hand, dismissing her, and concentrated on the game, yelling advice, as indeed was everyone else. Someone handed him a hip-flask of brandy, and he took a long swallow before handing it back with a smile of appreciation.

A roar of excitement went up from the crowd as fifteen minutes later Mareeba scored the winning goal barely seconds before time. But still it was not all over, and Marisa watched as Cesare hobbled on to the field, assisted by Alan and Fred Bombardi, to have team photographs taken.

'*Grazie*, Fred,' Cesare said some ten minutes later as he slid into the passenger seat of his car. 'Marisa will drive,' he indicated with a sweep of his arm in her direction.

What? Drive that huge thing? Heavens, she'd never driven anything other than the Mini!

'Come on, Marisa,' he commanded curtly through the window, and she hopped in behind the wheel like a scalded cat.

'Cesare, I can't drive this, I've never——' she began, her eyes large with incredulity.

'You can, and you will. *Dio Santo*, it's automatic transmission, all you've got to do is start the thing and drive! For heaven's sake, child, adjust the seat!' he bit out through clenched teeth.

She searched for the lever, and the next second the seat shot forward.

'*Dio Madonna!*' he cursed, gripping her seat with both hands. 'Push the lever,' he bade curtly, and she shakily did so. The seat moved slightly. 'Right,' he breathed, and she had the distinct impression that he was counting to ten. Carefully and precisely he instructed her, and lo and behold the car moved backwards. So far, so good. She adjusted the transmission gently and moved the car slowly towards the gate.

'To the left, here,' he muttered tersely, easing his foot slightly.

She drove cautiously as he directed the way to the hospital, and breathed a sigh of heartfelt relief when she parked the car close to the entrance in the hospital grounds. Hastily she slid out to help him hobble up the steps, which was achieved in a series of hops with time out to lean against her rather feeble support. They made it into the waiting-room, and from there the nursing staff took over. Details were taken, and he was commanded—if anyone could command *him*—into a wheelchair, and whisked away down a corridor.

In a short space of time the waiting-room filled with the entire Mareeba soccer team plus an anxious supporter or two. It seemed an age before a nurse appeared and indicated that Marisa should accompany her down the corridor to the men's ward.

Marisa felt the customary knot of tension at the sight of him, as incompatible with his surroundings as a mountain lion behind bars. She smiled at him tentatively, shy of the many eyes watching with avid interest from their beds.

'Does it hurt very much?' she enquired politely, anxiously searching the forceful lines of his rough-hewn features, rapidly moving her gaze as she caught the gleam in the depths of those dark brown eyes.

With a careless shrug he reached into the drawer of the cabinet beside his bed and withdrew his wallet. 'Be a good girl, and get me two packets of cigarettes. You'd better check the petrol in the car, too, it needs filling up.'

Marisa took the wallet from him and put it carefully into her shoulder bag, then nervously fingered her hair. 'I'll collect some of your things from the hotel as well, I suppose they've already served the patients' dinner,' she ventured with concern. 'Can I bring you something from the café?'

Cesare shook his head in refusal. 'No, I'm sure they can find something for me in the kitchen, in any case

I'm not particularly hungry.' He reached for his cigarettes and extracted the last one from the packet and lit it. 'Are you sure you can manage the car?' he queried lazily through a haze of smoke.

'Yes,' she answered with assurance, knowing she would handle it all the better without him there to criticise.

'The hotel's key to our room is in the zip compartment of the wallet. It looks as if they're going to ask you to go—here's the nurse,' he intoned quietly, and Marisa turned to see the nurse almost at her side.

'I'm sorry, Mrs Gianelli, I must ask you to leave now,' the nurse said with efficiency, and turned to Cesare. 'You seem to have a number of friends in the waiting-room. I've had to insist that they come back at visiting time. Also, we've managed to get a meal organised for you, it shouldn't be long.' She stood by silently, obviously waiting for Marisa to leave.

Marisa hesitated briefly, then impulsively leant forward and planted a shy butterfly kiss on his temple. For the benefit of the nurse and those attentively watchful men patients, she assured herself as she straightened and sketched a wave. Cesare's dark eyes glitered with amusement as she hurriedly turned and left the ward. Damn him! He knew very well she had done that for the sake of appearances!

The car responded beautifully, and she managed the drive back to the hotel without a hitch. Remembering Cesare's words about the petrol, she drove into a garage and had them fill the tank, and while she was there bought cigarettes.

At the hotel she managed to slip quietly upstairs, and she quickly collected his shaving gear, pyjamas, and anything else she thought he might want. There, that should do, she thought speculatively. Now to get back to the hospital with them.

Fred Bombardi hailed her as she crossed the hallway on her way out, and she assured him that Cesare would be in hospital overnight only, and that the fracture was a simple one.

'That is good,' he breathed a great sigh of relief.

'You tell him, please, that I come soon to see him. Most of the players, they come too, I know. We'll be there, half-past seven—you tell him, yes?' he said anxiously, and she assured him she would.

Cesare looked impatient and decidedly restless as Marisa appeared in the ward, and she thought it highly likely the ankle was giving him considerable pain.

'Did you remember the cigarettes?' he greeted her without preamble, and she handed them over silently, watching as he extracted one and lit it, exhaling the smoke with satisfaction.

'I've brought a few things I thought you might need,' she said quietly, and crossed round to the other side of the bed and knelt down to put them in his locker. She looked up from her task to relay Fred Bombardi's message, and he nodded absently.

'Have you had dinner yet?'

She shook her head. 'No, not yet. I'll get them to send something up when I get back to the hotel. I'm not very hungry, really, some sandwiches and coffee will do.' She stood to her feet and fastened the overnight bag as the first visitor entered the ward.

'As you like,' he shrugged, then glanced at his watch. 'You'd better get back, the others will be here soon. You'd better check out of the hotel, too, the account's already fixed up, and if you need a hand with anything, ask Fred—all right?' He stubbed out his cigarette and regarded her enigmatically. 'I'll see you in the morning.'

'Yes,' she replied dutifully, totally unprepared as he reached out to grasp her arms and pull her towards him. His lips were firm and warm as they met hers, savouring the cool sweetness of her mouth lingeringly before releasing her.

'Don't play games with me, *carina*,' he said softly. 'You're way out of your depth!'

Marisa's eyes widened and she hurriedly took a few steps away from his side to stand at the end of the bed. Cesare smiled musingly, his dark eyes twinkling at her confusion.

'You're—impossible!' she almost choked on the words, increasingly aware of a dozen pairs of interested eyes centred around them.

'Undoubtedly,' he agreed urbanely as he unhurriedly withdrew a cigarette and placed it in his mouth. A match flared as he lit it with studied ease, and his teeth gleamed as he directed a slow warm, almost gentle smile her way.

'*Ciao*, Marisa.'

She murmured something incoherent, and escaped out into the corridor. 'Really! Impossible wasn't the word! Certainly, he was the most unpredictable person she had ever met.

Shortly after nine o'clock next morning there was a knock at her door, and when she opened it Fred Bombardi stood hesitantly in the doorway.

'Good morning, *signora*. Everything is all right?' he queried, looking quite concerned.

Marisa nodded. 'Yes, thank you.'

His head bobbed up and down and he spread his hands outwards. 'I didn't see you at breakfast, I worry maybe something is wrong. Gianelli, he ask me to look after you, so I come to see.' He was relieved to have got it off his chest, and Marisa smiled gently at him.

'That's very kind of you,' she said gratefully as he stood there rather awkwardly.

'The players, they all go up last night to the hospital. Gianelli, he look not too bad, eh?'

'Yes, not too bad,' she agreed. 'I expect he'll be glad to get out of hospital.'

'Oh, *si*,' he agreed quickly, chuckling. '*Si*, that is for sure.' He made a slight shrugging gesture, lifting his shoulders fractionally, at the same time moving his hands a short distance outwards away from his sides. 'Well,' he smiled kindly, 'if there is nothing that I can do for you, I go. *Ciao*.'

'*Ciao*,' Marisa bade him, pleased with her first attempt at the Italian word. Hmmn, it sounded fine, and she repeated it again to herself as she shut the door.

It was almost ten minutes before ten as she parked

the car outside the hospital and made her way into the men's ward with Cesare's suitcase in her hand. The Sister on duty came to meet her with a hand outstretched for the case.

'Mrs Gianelli? I'll take this through to him, and perhaps you wouldn't mind waiting here,' she indicated some chairs against the corridor wall just outside the ward. 'We'll have to slit the seam of his trousers, I'm afraid, to accommodate the cast on his ankle. Now,' she said briskly, 'he already has the letter for the hospital in Mareeba, some pain tablets, and,' she went on severely, pursing her lips, 'he must be persuaded to rest the ankle each day. I cannot stress too much the necessity for this.' She gave a tight little smile, then turned abruptly away.

Marisa entertained no doubts that Cesare had proved a difficult patient; they were probably glad to be rid of him, she perceived wryly.

It was all of fifteen minutes before the Sister appeared with Cesare swinging along with ease on crutches behind her.

Marisa jumped to her feet, smoothing a stray lock of hair back behind her ear in a purely nervous gesture. She had left it loose this morning, having washed it beneath the shower earlier, and a few damp tendrils curled away and escaped to lie at will against the smooth golden skin of her throat. The black slacks, flared with a wide cuff at the ankle, accentuated her breathtaking slimness and the skinny-rib knit short-sleeved jumper with its bold wide stripes of black, red and gold was a perfect foil for her lightly tanned skin and honey-gold hair.

'Hello,' she greeted Cesare quietly, giving him a slight smile, and coloured beneath his careful scrutiny. Perhaps, after all, she should have worn a dress, she reflected ruefully, but with several hours' driving ahead of her slacks had seemed the obvious choice.

The Sister handed Marisa the suitcase, then cast Cesare a severe look.

'You will remember to rest that ankle, Mr Gianelli? It will be you who suffers,' she said briskly, and her tone intimated she had no doubt his wife would suffer too. Marisa thought grimly that she was probably right!

She walked beside Cesare as he thumped and swung himself along the passage and down the steps to the car. After depositing the suitcase in the boot, she slid in behind the wheel feeling distinctly nervous.

'You've checked out of the hotel, everything's in the boot?' he queried as he slid his leg into a more comfortable position.

'Yes,' she answered monosyllabically, concentrating on moving the large car out from its parking place.

'Good,' he intoned brusquely. 'Stop at a hotel, Marisa. I need a drink.'

Carefully she drove into the town, and as she parked outside a hotel she breathed an inaudible sigh of relief. No critical remarks so far!

Cesare reached over into the back seat for his crutches. 'Stay here, I won't be long,' he said curtly, and hopped out on to the pavement, then swung his way towards the hotel bar.

It was all of thirty minutes before he emerged, and as he slid into the car beside her he seemed to be in a better frame of mind.

'We'll call into the cane farm on our way out. My manager, Rafael Mendoza, knows I'm in town and will expect us for lunch,' he informed her, slanting a slow warm smile in her direction. 'You manage the car very well,' he complimented, 'even if you do look ridiculous perched behind the wheel.'

She shot him a baleful glance. 'I can't help my size, any more than you can,' she assured him indignantly.

'Neither you can, *nina*,' he placated soothingly. 'Now,' he swept his arm forward, indicating she should set the car moving, 'it's about ten miles off the main highway. Keep on this road until I direct you to turn off it.' He leant forward and switched on the car radio. Music, that was a relief, she wouldn't need to search for something to say!

It took little more than twenty minutes to reach the farm, and Marisa viewed the towering cane with awe as she parked the car in the yard beside the farmhouse.

An amply porportioned middle-aged woman came running towards them, her arms outstretched to welcome them profusely.

'Gianelli! *Madre de Dio!* What 'ave you done?' she raised her hands above her head in horror at the sight of his ankle in its plaster cast and the crutches on which he was leaning.

'*Signorina,*' she acknowledged, with a brief smile in Marisa's direction.

'Maria, meet my wife, Marisa,' Cesare introduced with a slight grin in Marisa's direction.

Maria gasped, and clapped her hands to her face in an eloquent gesture of disbelief.

'You marry? Ai-aye-ai!' she wailed, throwing her hands in the air. 'Why you no tell us, eh? Gianelli, you keep it quiet, eh? She,' she paused to catch Marisa's hands in hers, 'she look a beautiful girl, young,' she nodded her head several times and smiled widely, 'and ver-ry nice.'

Marisa felt the blush steal over her cheeks at such close scrutiny and Maria nodded her head again as if satisfied about something.

'Come inside, come inside, what we stand here for? Come on,' she beckoned briskly, and led the way up the steps on to the long verandah that seemed to go all the way round the outside of the house. 'Come on, come inside,' she indicated to Marisa to pass through into the large kitchen.

Cesare swung his way in and pulled out a chair and sat down, hooking another chair out with one of his crutches to rest his ankle on. Maria bustled in after them and pulled out a chair for Marisa.

'Sit down, sit down, Marisa. I just get the wine and some glasses, and we drink together.' She turned and gathered glasses from the cupboard on to the table, and took a half-gallon flagon of wine, dark red wine, and poured till the glasses were filled.

Marisa wondered if she could decently refuse the whole glass, and knew that she couldn't without insulting Maria's hospitality. Ai-aye-ai, she silently repeated Maria's words of a few moments ago!

Maria lifted her glass, 'Your health, and many fine sons,' and Cesare shot Marisa a wicked look, and drank almost half the contents of his glass to that. Marisa took a sip and tasted the coarse dry wine, and tried not to show her dislike of it.

'Now, you tell me what happen,' Maria indicated Cesare's ankle with a sweep of her arm. He smiled slightly, partly at Marisa's discomfiture over Maria's toast, and partly because he knew she disliked the wine.

'The other player and I were at grips over the ball,' he began to explain, shrugging negligently, 'and this,' he indicated his ankle, 'got in the way.'

Maria threw her hands heavenward. 'It is bad, yes?' she queried.

'No, not bad, just damned awkward,' Cesare revealed, drawing out cigarettes and matches from the breast pocket of his shirt.

'Rafael, he be in soon. You excuse, please?' she stood up and moved towards the stove. 'Everything, it is ready, almost. I just get it all from the saucepans now on to the plates.'

'Can I help you?' Marisa questioned, anxious to be away from the table and Cesare's quizzical teasing eyes.

'No, no, you stay there. The table is set, there is nothing to do, except for me. Ah,' Maria breathed, 'here is Rafael.'

Rafael was typically Spanish, in that he was slightly below average height, dark-skinned, and had dark gleaming expressive eyes. He greeted Cesare like a long-lost brother, and after the back-slapping petered out, Marisa was eventually introduced. This, naturally, necessitated a further toast, and to say the wine flowed like water was no exaggeration. Maria placed bowl after bowl of food on the table. There was paella, chicken, two different salads, something spicy with tomatoes and green and red peppers which Marisa tasted, and then promptly reached for her glass. Man, was it hot! Cesare ate hungrily, with obvious enjoyment, washing every second mouthful down with wine, as did Rafael and even Maria. The meal was a fairly leisurely one, and when it was finished the two men rose and went outside.

Maria filled the sink with hot sudsy water while Marisa cleared the table, stacking the dishes in orderly piles on the bench.

'Dishes, dishes—ai-aye-ai, always the dishes!' Maria complained goodnaturedly. 'The cooking, I no mind. The eating, I enjoy. But the dishes, maybe when I die they invent something, and the dishes they are no more!' she exclaimed, and lifted a sudsy hand high in the air.

Marisa laughed, and gathered up a tea-towel. 'I know what you mean. I have plenty now, and there are only four workers.'

Maria cleaned the plates in one sink and placed them into another to rinse, then stacked them in the dish-drainer on the bench.

'You like the farm, yes?' she queried with a quick appraising look at the girl by her side.

'Yes,' enthused Marisa, her eyes lighting up with pleasure as she thought of the lovely home standing so solid and secure on ground rich with red-brown sandy loam, the tall fresh-green plants planted in neat rows covering acre upon acre, the poultry pens with their squawking cackling broods. One day, at the end of the season, she would plant flowers all around the house in a wide border. Then, indeed, it would be *home*.

'That is good,' Maria nodded. 'In a few years it is even better. Cesare, he have the sons for the farm, and you, you have the daughters to help in the kitchen, and everything, she is all right. Life is good, yes?' she concluded with several nods, smiling widely at Marisa.

Marisa nodded, and managed a strangled reply.

Maria tackled a saucepan with vigour and scrubbed until it was shining bright.

'You like children, yes, lots of children?' Maria continued as she attacked yet another saucepan.

Marisa wondered rather wildly where the conversation would end. Maria had her with four children, at least, already, before she had even had a chance to conceive one of them!

'Yes, I like children,' she said quietly, and dried the plate in her hand rather more briskly than was required.

'Good, good,' Marisa nodded, and eyed her critically. Marisa felt inclined to be rash, and say she intended having at least six, or maybe eight children, *at least*!

'There,' breathed Maria with a sigh. 'They are all done. We make coffee now—the men, I see them coming.'

Cesare was in a hurry to get away, and did not linger any longer than was necessary over their coffee.

On the main highway he switched on the car radio and settled himself into a comfortable position and closed his eyes.

'Wake me when we get to Cairns,' he instructed lazily.

He slept as Marisa drove, and he didn't stir until they were approaching the outskirts of Cairns. The hills rose darkly against the clear evening light, fading rapidly now, and the air held a tingling freshness which was cool and sweet. Above those hills, on the plateau, several miles westward, lay the farm—and home. As she drove towards the Kuranda Range, an hour later and after a relaxing dinner in one of Cairns' restaurants, her heart lifted with a wondrous feeling of happy contentment. The powerful beam of the car's headlights probed the darkness as the ribbon of asphalt rose, winding upwards through heavily bushed foliage, then gradually straightening, stretching out far into the inky blackness of the night leading her homeward.

As she brought the car to a halt in the yard beside their home Carlo and Rosa came out to welcome them, clicking their tongues as they commiserated over Cesare's ankle and evincing their delight that Mareeba had won the coveted Grazioli Shield.

Marisa put the car away as Cesare disappeared into the bulking shed with Carlo, then skipped up the steps into the brightly lit kitchen. She took the two suitcases Carlo had deposited inside only minutes before and began unpacking them, her mind moving agilely over the things she must do before going to bed. There was meat to be taken from the deep-freeze, bread too, and the dust must be wiped from the furniture and swept from the floors. It was all of forty minutes before she stepped under the steamy hot needle-spray of the shower and flexed the stiff muscles of her arms and shoulders tired from driving. Bed was a welcome sight, and she slipped in between the crisp sheets breathing a sigh of pure contentment.

CHAPTER NINE

THE first few days Cesare was very irritable because his ankle prevented him from working for very long at anything, although he insisted on driving the tractor to and from the paddock. He refused to rest for more than an hour during the afternoon, and was brusque with everyone. Marisa kept her tongue in cheek, and only spoke when spoken to. She thought he was well aware that she was keeping out of his way, for once or twice she caught sight of a twinkle in those dark eyes as they regarded her thoughtfully.

There was a letter from Tony waiting at the post office when she checked on Wednesday morning, and she ripped it open anxiously. Everything was fab, from the teachers to the subjects in his curriculum. He'd been selected for the first team at cricket, and had done well at the swimming trials. The only drawback was the food, which was unimaginative, he relayed, but apart from that he was enjoying college to the utmost. Marisa gave a great sigh of relief as she re-folded the letter—thank heavens for that!

She braved the poultry pen that afternoon, and managed to capture three chickens without any fuss, and decided while she was about it, she might as well attempt two young ducks as well. Fired with enthusiasm, she plucked them all and took them inside to disembowel, a task she hated utterly and performed with caution.

Unfortunately, Cesare came into the kitchen just as she was about to begin, and stood there watching critically. Head bent, she resolved not to take any notice of him as she gingerly began on the first fowl. Yuk. She'd *never* get used to this!

'God forbid, girl!' he deplored impatiently. 'Don't play around with the thing, get stuck into it!'

Her cheeks warmed with colour as she bit her lip, feeling the prick of tears in her eyes.

'A ten-year-old could do better than that,' he scorned as he swung on his crutches to stand beside her, dwarfing her as he towered head and shoulders above her. 'Here,' he edged her out of the way, taking the offending bird with one hand. 'Like this,' he demonstrated, and put it to one side, reaching for the second bird, 'and this,' giving a grunt of satisfaction as the job was cleanly completed. 'Now, you do it.'

She shot him a doubtful look from beneath her lashes as he moved to one side. 'Are you going to stay and watch?'

'I am,' he assured her indisputably as he washed his hands.

Oh dear, he darned well would! Of all the domineering, arrogant, self-assured——!

'Stop swearing at me underneath your breath, and get on with it,' he commanded imperatively.

Well! Marisa grabbed one bird and quite quickly completed the task, and was reaching for the duck when the sound of a car pulling into the yard caused her to look out the window.

'Looks as though we've got company,' Cesare indicated calmly, and swung and thumped his way out to the door. Hurriedly she washed the three chickens and thrust them into plastic bags ready for the freezer.

A girl's light laughter reached her, and she turned to see Tania in the dining-room with Cesare looming behind her.

'Tania!' Marisa smiled with pleasure as she dried her hands on her apron.

'Hi there,' Tania wandered into the kitchen and grinned at her. 'You look a bit flustered—has he been getting at you?' she enquired cheekily, and tilted her head up at Cesare. 'Shame on you,' she chastised. 'She's half your size, and twice as nice. Ah—hah!' she breathed as she caught sight of the ducks on the bench. 'Your first efforts?' Her bright eyes sparkled as she turned towards Marisa.

'Can't say I blame you feeling squeamish. It's not exactly a task one takes to willingly, is it? Here,' she rinsed her hands under the tap and took hold of one of the ducks, 'I'll finish off for you.' And with a dexterity Marisa couldn't help but admire, Tania whisked and rinsed, wrapped and disposed of the remaining birds and their remains.

'There,' she smiled bewitchingly from Marisa to Cesare, who, much to Marisa's surprise and relief, threw back his head and roared with laughter. She silently blessed Tania for her timely arrival and pert humour.

'I can see I'm outnumbered nicely. I'll be in the bulking shed,' he chuckled as he swung his way out of the kitchen.

Tania winked at Marisa wickedly. 'Before you go, you can accept the family's invitation to dinner on Sunday, yes?'

Cesare turned slightly as he opened the screen-door. 'Thanks, we'll be there, yes. *Ciao,*' he bade her, letting the screen-door bang behind him.

Tania turned to Marisa, her expression assuming an efficient look. 'Now, before we start talking and lose track of time, is it your smoko this afternoon?'

Marisa nodded, 'Yes, but everything's ready except for the tea.' She undid her apron and put it over the back of one of the chairs, smiling at Tania ruefully. 'Thanks for doing the ducks for me. I don't think I'll ever get used to it.'

Tania laughed and tossed her dark hair back over her shoulders. 'Of course you will. In another three months you won't turn a single hair, I'm willing to bet on it.'

Marisa wrinkled her nose and grinned ruefully. 'I doubt it. Will you have some coffee?'

'Mmmn, love some.' Tania pulled out a chair and sat down. 'Nothing to eat, Marisa, I had a huge lunch.'

Marisa set the percolator on to heat and took down two cups and saucers.

'Has Cesare told you about the barbecue, Saturday week?'

Marisa looked up with surprise. 'No, not yet.'

'It's an annual event. End of the soccer season's celebration,' Tania continued, 'only this year more so, as we've won the coveted Shield. There'll be champagne, no less, and no doubt it'll go on till dawn.'

Marisa poured the steaming coffee into cups and carried them to the table.

'There'll be dancing, they get a jolly good band,' Tania enlightened her, 'and steaks, hamburgers, you name it, and beer by the kegful. Everyone goes.' Her face had come alive and her eyes glowed. Marisa smiled with delighted anticipation.

'It sounds great. What does a girl wear—slacks, or a dress?'

Tania contrived to look horrified. 'Good lord, dear girl, don't wear slacks! We're dreadfully old-fashioned in this neck of the woods. Nothing less than one of your best dresses will do!'

Marisa's wide mouth curved sheepishly. 'Oh dear, I have put my foot in it!'

Tania threw up her hands in mock indignation. 'Have you ever!' She sipped her coffee and smiled across the table at Marisa. 'You feel like a fish out of water among all this, don't you?' she enquired kindly.

Marisa looked startled, and searched for an answer that was non-committal. 'It's very—different from working in an office,' she began, trying to meet Tania's clear gaze.

'I envy you,' Tania said suddenly.

Marisa put her cup back on to its saucer with care.

'Do you?' she answered politely, wondering what was coming next.

'It must be great to get out and work, not to have to stay at home.' Tania looked at Marisa enviously. 'Oh, if you only knew how much I'd give to be able to get a job!'

Marisa looked taken aback, her hazel eyes widening as she regarded the girl across the table. 'Are you still at school? I thought you——'

Tania shook her head impatiently. 'I left school four years ago,' she interrupted. 'I'm *twenty*!' Her expressive face was deadly earnest. 'Papa will have me married off at the end of the season if he can manage it, and Mother just shrugs her shoulders in despair of me!' She managed a rueful grin, her deep grey eyes a little sad. 'Sorry to have unburdened myself, but you're different. At least you haven't been brought up with an immemorial tradition hammered into your head.' She raised her eyes heavenward. 'Oh, for the day Women's Lib reaches us!' She finished her coffee and leaned on the table.

'You'll see what I mean when you meet the family on Sunday. I have one brother and two sisters, all married, and all very much in favour of getting *me* married off. I probably shall, just for the sake of peace!'

Marisa laughed, and looked at the other girl with amusement. 'I can't imagine you being forced to do anything you weren't agreeable to.'

Tania grinned wickedly. 'Oh, *forced* isn't the right word. It's more a combination of high pressure salesmanship and gentle persuasion. If one doesn't work, the other will!' She glanced at her watch in dismay. 'Heavens, I must fly! I promised Mother I'd be back by three.' She scrambled to her feet and tucked her chair under the table.

'It's been lovely to see you, Tania,' Marisa said impulsively. 'Do come again soon.'

Tania smiled and touched Marisa's hand. 'I will, perhaps next week. Anyway, I'll see you on Sunday. *Ciao*.' She opened the screen-door and ran lightly down the steps to the car.

'*Ciao*,' Marisa called, waving as the car reversed and sped swiftly down the drive.

Cesare seemed in a better frame of mind over the next few days. He spent most of his time in the bulking shed, and on Friday morning insisted that Marisa take the car into Mareeba to collect all the meat and groceries for the next fortnight. He elected to come with her to find two more men for the farm. Marisa added to her list, and wondered if the boot of the car would hold it all. She hated to think what the total food bill for a season would amount to! All that meat! And she mustn't forget to get some more corn and mash for the poultry. Fish was the usual fare for a Friday evening meal, not because of any religious tradition, but because it was a habit that had something to do with the fishmonger's truck from Cairns being parked outside the Royal Hotel in Mareeba from eleven until twelve noon on a Friday morning!

The kitten, now weaned from its mother and one day in residence inside the house, mewed and rubbed its fluffy little body against Marisa's foot as she checked her list. She grinned down at it and murmured, 'Yes, Buffy, fish. You shall have some for your tea.'

'Ready?' Cesare's voice from the dining-room startled her.

'Yes, coming.' She thrust her list into her shoulder-bag and picked up the letter she had written to Tony the previous evening.

Cesare watched indulgently, a slight smile tugging at his lips as she put the kitten into its box by the sink. It was a rather large box with an old piece of blanket at one end, a plastic tray of dirt at the other, and fresh newspaper in between. Satisfied, she followed Cesare out to the car and slid behind the wheel.

'Go and do what shopping you want, and have some coffee or something,' Cesare suggested when she had parked the car outside the Graham Hotel in Mareeba. 'Leave your order with the butcher and the grocer, we'll pick it up on the way out.' He searched in his trouser pocket and withdrew a spare set of keys for the car which he handed to her. 'I'll need an hour, possibly longer, to rustle up a couple of men. Be back here by eleven, and wait for me.' With that he slid out from the car and swung his way across the pavement into the bar of the hotel.

A whole hour to wander round the shops—lovely! The post office first, to post Tony's letter, then the stationer's for a new pad and a magazine. And yes, she would go to a café and have a nice espresso coffee. Mmmm, such luxury!

The time passed all too quickly, and it was a few minutes after eleven when Cesare slid into the car beside her, an air of satisfaction to his manner as he lit the inevitable cigarette and blew smoke out of the window.

'Did you manage to get some men?' she queried as she eased the car back on to the road, then set it moving round the huge spreading trees in the centre of the street.

'Three. They've worked for me before. I'll come in tonight with Carlo and pick them up.'

Three! Would she have two, and Rosa one, or the other way around, or all three?

'By the way,' he continued calmly, 'after lunch, Rosa will show you how to string up. With three extra men picking, we'll need you to string. The meals come first, of course, you understand?' he quirked an eyebrow as he looked across at her.

She nodded and sighed a silent expressive 'ai-aye-ai'. One thing about it, there just wasn't time to brood about anything!

Lunch was a little late, and by the time she cleared the dishes, unpacked the groceries and meat, it was almost two o'clock. Oh, lord—it was her smoko, too!

With a haste that bordered on panic, she sliced bread and made sandwiches, placing everything in the wicker basket. The tea was in its gauze bag in the kettle awaiting the boiling water.

She almost ran across the yard to the verandah between the bulking shed and the barns. Rosa looked up, and beckoned her to the empty stringing-horse behind her.

'Sorry I'm late,' Marisa apologised, conscious of appraisal from several pairs of interested eyes, but Rosa merely smiled and began her instructions. The stick was quickly and skilfully strung, and Marisa almost ran to keep up with Rosa as she carried it across to the barn.

Each individual barn was square, approximately twenty feet in height and divided into sections by a structure of horizontal and vertical wooden beams. The sticks of strung tobacco were placed horizontally at regularly spaced intervals.

'You see? You follow on. One at the top, then next one down, then on the lower one. The men come in, smoko time, and lift them all up on to the top, then we fill the lower half again. Soon we pick two barns each day,' Rosa finished proudly.

Help! Marisa pleaded. If Rosa could manage it, she would. The important thing, she staunchly reminded herself, was not to lose one's sense of humour!

She managed to string three sticks, and very proudly too, before hurrying inside to boil water for the tea.

That evening she fell into bed with sore limbs, tender fingers, and a decidedly deflated ego.

Saturday dawned, and with it came two new faces for early morning coffee.

Marisa nodded as Cesare introduced them, her brain reeling ahead that if she sprinted through all her chores, she could be under the verandah, stringing up, by eight-fifteen.

What a day! And to cap it all, Cesare indicated that they would go into Mareeba to the pictures that evening.

Pictures! The only thing she wanted was her nice comfortable bed, as soon after dinner as she could decently get there!

Still, one had a reputation to make, and if almost everyone else went into town on a Saturday night, then go must she. Next Friday, she vowed, she would consult the local chemist for some vitamin pills to keep up her strength! And perhaps a course of salt tablets, as well!

The cinema was screening a double feature, but Marisa sat through the first half barely managing to keep her eyes open, and shortly afterwards gave in to the irresistible desire to doze. She lifted her head in surprise and confusion from its resting place against Cesare's shoulder as her arm was shaken gently.

'Come on, sleepy-head. Home time!' His breath was warm against her cheek, and she focused, recognising her surroundings, her eyes widening with disbelief and embarrassment.

'Oh, Cesare, I'm sorry,' her voice sounded slightly cracked with weariness.

His smile was curiously tender as he looked down at her, his face only inches from hers.

'You didn't miss a thing. Come on,' he stood grasping her hand and helping her to her feet. Almost in a dream she followed him out of the cinema to the car, acutely aware that her hand was firmly held in his. The alarm wouldn't go off till six-fifteen, as the following day was Sunday, and there wouldn't be any early morning coffee for the men. Bliss, absolute bliss!

To Marisa's delight, the men slid into their respective cars after breakfast and took off for places unknown, not to return until late evening. A day off, with only Cesare to cook lunch for, and yes, of course! They were to visit Tania's family for dinner. Hooray! It was like playing truant from school!

'Hi there,' Tania greeted them both enthusiastically. 'I've been watching out for you.'

Cesare raised a hand in greeting, then made his way towards the men gathered beneath the verandah drinking cans of beer and seemingly deep in earnest discussion.

'Come into the house, Marisa. There are a few other women there, and the men won't come in until dinner-time.'

Marisa walked beside her, feeling a little shy as

Tania led her through to the dining-room. The women sitting at the table looked up and smiled as Marisa was introduced. She accepted a cup of coffee from Mrs Petricevic, and concentrated on answering questions about herself without being too revealing, and after twenty minutes or so was grateful when Tania suggested that they go to her room as she wanted Marisa's opinion of a dress she had made.

It was a gay and chintzy room, in shades of pale lilac, pink and a smoky grey-blue. There were pin-ups of some pop stars on one wall, a crucifix over the head of the bed, and shelves of books alongside a large built-in wardobe.

Tania threw open the door of the wardobe and drew out a dress, holding it up for Marisa's inspection.

'What do you think of it? I copied it from a magazine, but Mother won't let me wear it. She reckons I look like a gypsy in it!' She laughed, and Marisa chuckled unrestrainedly. It certainly was way out in style, and scarcely what the respected daughter of strict Dalmatian parents could wear. It was long and flowing, with a low scooped-out neckline and puffed sleeves, with rows of shirring-elastic around the midriff.

'I wanted to wear it to the barbecue next Saturday night, but Mother put her foot down, and raised her hands to heaven that Papa should even *see* such a dress on me!'

Marisa felt the laughter bubble up inside her, feeling relaxed with this vitally alive, friendly girl.

'Perhaps, if you shortened it, you might get away with it. I think it's lovely, really, but for Cairns, or the cities further south. If the magazines are anything to go by, these styles are being worn everywhere.' She fingered the material, noting the expert finishing on the dress. 'Do you sew very much, Tania?'

The other girl made a deprecatory gesture. 'A little. I do sew for people, it's the only thing Papa will let me do, other than work on the farm.' She looked wistfully at Marisa. 'I'd have loved to work in a boutique, you know, learn the "ins and outs" of it, and take orders, and create original styles, but Papa says "no" most emphatically. If I *must* sew, I do do so at home, for pocket money. The farm comes first. I must help Mother cook for the men, help with the chores and string up.' She went on quickly. 'Papa pays me for stringing, of course, and he pays my accounts for materials, clothes and things, in town.' She grimaced wryly, 'I'm afraid he thinks the only fit career for me is marriage to someone he approves of, Nick Bragovic preferably.' She stopped speaking suddenly, and with a careless gesture flung the dress back into the wardrobe.

With a forced smile Tania turned back, and made Marisa look through some fashion magazines.

There was a full table that evening, for as well as Marisa and Cesare, there were Tania's brother Ivan and his wife Gianna, Tania's two sisters Anna and Luisa and their husbands, respectively Toni and George, four children, Mr and Mrs Petricevic, and two workers, plus a few others whose names Marisa could not remember.

There was ravioli, chickens, salads, home-baked bread rolls, and, of course, plenty of wine.

Cesare sat beside her, but apart from a cursory glance or two, he conversed with the men. Marisa noted that meals were not silent rituals with these people, and she was quick to realise that a Sunday evening dinner was an infinitely more leisurely affair than its weekday counterpart.

The men played cards at the dining-room table after dinner with companionable rowdiness, and it was close on midnight before they declared the game over and made a move towards leaving for their respective homes. As the days passed, each seemed to become more hectic, and apart from mealtimes Marisa saw Cesare very rarely. If he was not busy in the bulking shed, he was out in the paddock driving the tractor. His ankle didn't appear to bother him, or if it did, he made no comment. He used a single crutch now with an easy agility, and Marisa had long since given up worrying if he was doing his ankle any harm.

Her thoughts were occupied to the extent that sometimes a whole day would pass and she hadn't thought of Tony at all. But inevitably, when she did think of him, her thoughts slid on to Cesare and herself, and mercifully there was never much time to dwell on the situation. If it wasn't a meal to prepare, smoko, or stringing-up, there was a whole host of other things waiting to get done. She began to feel like the white rabbit in Lewis Carroll's *Alice,* forever on the run.

However, just after eight on Saturday evening, she was sitting in the car with Cesare, en route to Fred Bombardi's farm and the soccer barbecue. Her long skirt cascaded in silken flares to her feet, gaily patterned in bright psychedelic swirls of red, orange, black and green, on a multi-hued background of pale lilac deepening into wild purple. The halter-necked top in white jersey silk was demurely styled, and its ties wound round the waist and midriff were inches wide. There hadn't been a great deal of time to do anything outstanding with her hair, and in desperation she had back-combed part of it to give her a little added height and brought some hair forward to lie curling in long waves on her bosom.

Cesare looked formal in black tailored trousers, a dark blue silk shirt, and an even deeper navy-blue tie. His jacket was left casually unbuttoned, and Marisa suppressed an involuntary gasp at his appearance. He looked positively piratical!

'There's a fair crowd here already,' Cesare observed, locking the car and sweeping his arm in the direction of numerous vehicles gleaming darkly about them.

'Yes,' Marisa agreed quietly, feeling a little shy as she walked beside him into the artificial light under the enormous verandah. As they drew closer, heads lifted and arms waved in greeting.

'Hey, Gianelli! Come over here!' It was a good-hearted bellow, and echoed by several other voices.

Cesare smiled, and swung his way towards the makeshift bar of trestles running the length of the verandah.

'What'll you have? Beer, whisky, brandy, gin, Cinzano, rum?' Fred queried of Cesare. 'And you, *signora*?' he turned to Marisa.

'*Signora*. Hey, that's me!' she thought with amusement, intimating she would prefer a Cinzano with lemonade. Cesare chose beer, and as they stood Marisa idly glanced among the sea of people. She identified a few players, one of whom was Alan, and a few vaguely familiar faces. The band loudly proclaimed its presence in the bulking shed, and she mentally winced as the drummer attacked the cymbals with gay abandon.

'You are about to be rescued,' a voice erupted from behind, and she swung round to see Tania with her mother and father.

'Hi,' Marisa smiled with evident relief.

Tony Petricevic slapped Cesare's shoulder in greeting, and accepted a beer, but apart from a brief nod to Marisa the three women were totally ignored.

Tania threw up her hands in resignation, proclaiming 'Men!' in slightly disgusted tones, then caught hold of Marisa's arm and beckoned to her mother. 'We've lost them already! Come on, let's go inside,' and when Marisa looked doubtfully in Cesare's direction, Tania nudged Cesare's elbow and indicated they would be in the bulking shed with most of the other womenfolk.

Womenfolk was particularly apt, Marisa thought wryly a few minutes later, for the bulking shed was brightly lit and alive with chattering women sitting on forms and chairs placed around the walls—there were no men inside at all, except for the members of the band! They found some vacant chairs and sat down, and Tania kept up a running commentary on who was who as new faces appeared in twos and threes.

An hour or so later some of the younger men drifted inside to claim a dance with their respective wives or girl friends, then, duty done, disappeared quickly back to the bar. Shortly after eleven o'clock, Fred Bombardi announced that the food was ready and Marisa joined the leisurely file of women exiting from the bulking shed. The smell of sizzling steaks and sausages assailed her nostrils, and she had moved only a few paces towards the barbecue pit when Cesare and Tony Petricevic joined them.

'Enjoying yourself?' Cesare enquired lazily, and she nodded silently.

She was, but heavens, she fervently hoped it wouldn't be too long before they went home. She was so tired! Waiting for Cesare to get her steakburger, she stifled a yawn inconspicuously, feeling guilty. All these people worked just as hard as she, and yet they looked equal to at least another three or four hours of socialising. There was a large urn of steaming aromatic black coffee and numerous cups and saucers stacked at the end of one of the trestles, and Marisa weaved her way towards it, following Tania through the milling crowd. It was hot and sweet, and as Marisa sipped the strong brew she enjoyed its reviving effect.

'Look alive, there'll be all the speeches and presentations in a few minutes,' Tania informed her. 'You'll have a glass of champagne pushed into your tiny hand, and you'll have to salute the merits of each player in turn, plus the president of the club, the coach, team manager and the sponsor.' She grinned wickedly over the rim of her cup. 'Then, because they're so pleased with themselves, they'll condescend to dance till the witching hour of midnight when the band folds up. From then on, depending on how many drinks they have to have for the road, we women begin the process of prising them away from the bar for home sweet home.'

Marisa looked closely at her, seeing the tiny lines of strain pulling at the other girl's mouth. 'You're very—cynical, tonight,' she observed, and then tentatively enquired if anything was wrong.

Tania pulled a face, 'I finally bowed down to the combined pressure of my entire family this afternoon,' she sighed, her face suddenly taking on a petulant look, and her eyes flashed stormily.

'How do you mean?' Marisa enquired gently, looking concerned.

'I've consented to marry Nick Bragovic, from Melbourne, much to my parents' everlasting delight.

They've been at me long enough,' she grimaced wryly. 'For the last year, in fact.' She finished her coffee and replaced the cup on the trestle, turning back towards Marisa. 'I have been assured by my father,' she began ticking them off on her fingers, 'my mother, my brother, my two sisters, my sister-in-law and even my cousin Elena that if I refuse this time to marry him, no self-respecting son of any self-respecting family from our beloved old country will ever ask for me, and I shall be doomed to be a crotchety old maid, like Aunt Katija!' Her eyes sparkled dangerously. 'I feel like getting drunk,' she added inelegantly, and Marisa felt alarmed as she sought to soothe the girl at her side.

'Tania! Don't you want to get married—I mean, not at all?' she felt inclined to ask.

Tania sighed, then shrugged her shoulders expressively. 'Yes, I guess so. I quite like Nick, he's okay, I suppose,' she said matter-of-factly. 'I'm just not ready to settle down and produce a child with predictable regularity every eighteen months or so, that's all. At least, not yet. In any case, it's all very well for you. At least you've worked for your living, and led an independent life.' Tania eyed Marisa enviously. 'You had a choice, you could do your own thing. Me? I've had——'

Marisa interrupted as the other girl's voice rose bitterly. 'Tania, shhh! Your mother will hear you,' she cautioned.

Tania pulled a face, then took a deep breath, slowly. She flashed a smile that tore at Marisa's rather sensitive nature, for it was a bitter brittle smile, and quite spoilt her expression.

'Anyway, what the hell? A girl has to marry some time, and Nick is filthy rich,' she tossed her head defiantly. 'I shall see to it that I get an extravagant allowance, and take pleasure in spending every cent of it!' Her eyes flashed balefully, and Marisa felt at a loss what to say.

At that precise moment Marisa saw Cesare moving towards them. He towered over her, making her feel tiny beside his lofty height.

'They're nearly ready for the presentation now,' he indicated, handing her a glass of bubbly, and Marisa took it with a smile and turned towards Tania. The other girl murmured indistinctly and quickly slipped away.

Over the next hour there were speeches by the dozen, some short, some long, but each delivered with apparent good humour, and there was much laughter, back-slapping, and plenty of applause. The coveted Shield was raised to be viewed and applauded by all, and then a miniature was presented to each player in recognition of individual effort.

Marisa brushed back a lock of hair, blinking her eyes with conscious effort, and wondered how much longer it would be before Cesare would take her home. It was past midnight, surely the whole thing must wind up soon! But no, the band in the bulking shed struck up again with a gay bouncy tune that did little to revive her tired spirits.

'Another drink?' Cesare queried. He, bother him, didn't look the least bit weary. She shook her head, and concentrated on keeping her eyes open.

'*O Sole Mio*', one voice at the far end of the verandah began tentatively, joined within seconds by at least ten other voices, and as each cadence progressed, so did the volume. The band was lost, drowned out, and after several minutes the group of five musicians gave up, and disbanded.

The womenfolk slowly gathered together as the men drifted towards the steadily increasing group of singers, lifting their eyebrows at each other in expressive resignation as their menfolk followed one song with another. Every so often the men gave their voices the fortification of a quickly quaffed brandy, or rum, or whisky—or whatever. Some were almost rocking on their feet from the combined effects of alcohol and a day's hard toil, and some had partially collapsed and were leaning against the nearest wall. But they still sang, Marisa observed, and the liquor still flowed.

'I'm so tired,' she assured herself, 'that I shall go to sleep standing on my feet, and when I fall down, perhaps then Cesare will take me home. I'm sure I can't keep my eyes open one second longer.'

'What did you say?' She blinked slowly. Had she really spoken her thoughts aloud?

'Come and sit down, over here,' Cesare bent low as he spoke into her ear, and even then he scarcely made himself heard above the noise. She followed him a short distance and, dreamlike, was pulled down and gently held against his side by a massive imprisoning arm. Oh, the bliss of being able to lean against something! She was past caring about anything, and even if she had the will, she didn't possess the strength to keep her eyes open.

It seemed only seconds later that Cesare was bending over her, shaking her awake. 'Come on, child, wake up!'

She stared almost sightlessly at the face so close to her own, and clutched at the hard hands on her arms.

'Marisa!'

Slowly she shook her head, and feeling slightly dazed stood to her feet, swaying a little. A hand grasped her arm as Cesare steadied her, then he stood up beside her and caught her hand in his. To her surprise the singing was still in full voice, and there seemed a large number of people still present.

She shivered as they left the warm atmosphere of the verandah for the cool night air surrounding the cars. With a weariness that almost numbed her, she slid into the passenger seat and laid her head back against the cushioned vinyl, scarcely aware of the car's movement as it sped swiftly homewards.

CHAPTER TEN

MARISA and Cesare entertained their first guests for dinner the following Sunday. Not given to doing things by halves, Cesare informed her that no less than the entire Petricevic family plus a few other guests were invited. Marisa did swift mental calculations and came up with eleven adults and four children—and while she was still trying to catch her startled breath, he added that it was likely three of the workers would stay in for dinner as well.

'My, oh my!' was all she could think of to utter right then, and spent two practically sleepless nights planning a menu and worrying over the correct amount of spaghetti to cook and the number of chickens to prepare.

Despite her steadily rising panic all through Sunday morning that the meal would *never* be on time, and she had better kill at *least* another two chickens, the moment the Petricevic womenfolk stepped through the door in the early afternoon the majority of the remaining preparations were whisked competently out of her protesting hands.

In a whirl of organisation, Marisa learnt that Tania's engagement party was scheduled for the following Saturday night. Nick Bragovic was flying up from Melbourne on Thursday and would spend approximately ten days in Mareeba before returning south, and in all probability would not return again until a few days before the wedding, which at this stage was tentatively set for March.

'What do you think of a Victorian style, for my wedding dress, I mean?' Tania queried, as Marisa undid packets of spaghetti at the table in the kitchen.

'Oh, honestly, Tania, stick to something conventional!' Luisa reproved as she shot her mother a hasty look. Mrs Petricevic pursed her lips and shook her head in a gesture of frustration.

Marisa tried to be diplomatic, a worried frown creasing her forehead as she broke the spaghetti into shorter lengths. 'It would depend what you had in mind,' she answered prudently. 'Personally, I prefer something classical, in a heavy delustred satin, perhaps. It's such a rich material, it doesn't need flounces or frills to set it off.'

Tania grimaced wryly. 'Say, whose side are you on, anyway?' Her grin was friendly, but her eyes were bright and Marisa had a feeling she was deliberately being perverse just for the hell of it.

'Yes,' Mrs Petricevic nodded in agreement, 'that is what I tell her, but,' she shrugged a trifle wearily, 'she seems to want to be difficult, about—everything!'

'Look, Mother,' Tania turned towards her, eyeing her balefully. 'It's my wedding, and I'll wear what I like. If you don't all stop *getting* at me, I'll wear a mini-skirt and a see-through blouse,' she threatened darkly, with a hint of truculence.

Luisa finished washing the last lettuce leaf, and turned from the sink to face Tania. 'I hope to God Nick beats you, you ungrateful wretch. I'm sure if he had an inkling how self-willed you are, he'd call the whole thing off!'

Tania's eyes flashed. 'Oh, belt up!'

'Tania! Luisa! Stop this at once,' Mrs Petricevic exclaimed in horror, her eyes wide with distress.

Anna fetched a large pail of freshly peeled and washed potatoes from the bench and placed them on the table beside Marisa.

'She's a rebel, is our Tania,' she related with a hint of exasperation.

Marisa smiled slightly and shook her head in disbelief. 'Oh, surely not.'

The other girl snorted impatiently. 'She's been spoilt from the day she was born, premature and such a cute wee scrap,' Anna sighed reflectively. 'She's held Papa and Ivan in the palm of her hand ever since. Luisa and I were never permitted such latitude. Oh, well,' she continued perfunctorily, 'let's hope Nick can handle her, for she's a regular little spitfire at times.'

Marisa glanced quickly at Mrs Petricevic and suggested coffee in an attempt to divert the conversation.

'Yes, that would be nice,' the older woman breathed gratefully, while Tania and Luisa continued to look daggers at each other.

The screen-door banged loudly in that instant, and one of the children darted into the kitchen.

'Mamma, Mamma!' Luisa's youngest son, Marin, ran to his mother's side and clung desperately to her arm.

'Hush, child, what *is* the matter?' Luisa held him

away and looked down into his tear-stained face, but the child was beside himself and she could get no sense out of him at all.

'Marin!' roared his father, thundering into the kitchen, the wrath of God, no less, emanating from his powerful frame.

The boy cringed closer against his mother, and buried his head in her bosom. Luisa looked askance at her husband, but he took not a scrap of notice of the entreaty in her glance.

'Outside,' he ordered vociferously, '*pronto*!'

Marisa saw with concern the boy's figure twitch with fear. He was barely seven years old, surely whatever he was guilty of, it didn't warrant this public display.

Luisa made a conciliatory gesture towards her husband. 'George,' she began tentatively, but he waved his arm in anger.

'Be quiet, Luisa. Outside, Marin,' his voice was quieter, but the threat of impending punishment was evident, and at a gentle push from his mother, Marin placed one foot in front of the other and preceded his father out of the kitchen.

The door banged shut behind them, and the girls eyed each other expressively. Marisa let out the breath she had unconsciously held over the past few seconds, and set the percolator on the radiant plate. Poor little Marin, she thought sympathetically, as she set cups on saucers and withdrew the sugar bowl from the cupboard. These men, they threw themselves into everything with complete wholeheartedness. Nothing, she pondered ruefully, was ever done casually.

Over coffee, as they sat round the lower end of the dining-room table, the colour, style and choice of material for Tania's dress for her engagement party were bandied between her mother and sisters. Marisa gave her opinion when asked, but otherwise determined to maintain a safe neutrality on the subject. It seemed a deep gold polyester crêpe had everyone's approval, and only Mrs Petricevic was unenthusiastic over the style Tania had chosen. Fortunately the matter was temporarily shelved as it was time to turn the chickens in the oven, check the potatoes, and set a huge pan of water boiling for the spaghetti.

The meal was an outstanding success. Flushed and happy, Marisa witnessed the evident enjoyment with which everyone ate their dinner, and felt unaccountably relieved that there was plenty of food and that she hadn't miscalculated quantities, after all. She caught Cesare's eye on one of the occasions she scanned the table, and was immediately arrested by the appreciative, almost loving smile he gave her. Her stomach somersaulted slowly as she wrestled with her emotions, reasoning despondently that it had been for appearances' sake, that rather wonderful smile.

After dinner, Tania seemed to retire into a mood of introspection, declining to converse with anyone, and it was fortunate that the men chose to play cards at the dining-room table. Marisa had a shrewd suspicion Tania's moodiness would not have been permitted to prevail in their presence.

It was very late when the womenfolk managed to persuade their respective husbands it was time to go home. The children were scooped up from beds, wrapped in blankets ready to be deposited in their parents' cars, and Marisa stood at Cesare's side smiling as she bid everyone a charmingly accented '*buona notte*'.

As the last car disappeared from the yard she turned back into the dining-room, pleasantly tired and filled with well-being that all had gone as it should. That, praise be, she had carried it off better than she had hoped! She ran hot water into the sink to deal with the numerous empty glasses and coffee cups, and heard the screen-door click as Cesare shut and locked the back door.

She stiffened slightly, feeling the tension knot in her stomach as he moved into the kitchen to stand behind her.

'Goodnight, *carina*,' he murmured softly, and she felt the warmth of his fingers against the soft skin at the back of her neck as he swept the thick swathe of hair aside.

'Oh, stop it, please. Don't—*please* don't mix me up

any more than I am already,' she begged silently at the touch of his lips against her neck. It was almost more than she could bear not to lean back against that broad chest and seek the refuge of his embrace.

'Sleep well, child.' Her hair received a gentle tug, and endless seconds later she heard him leave the kitchen.

There was a card from Tony on Thursday, together with a newsy letter from Brenda. Marisa smiled a little as she read it, for the replacement at the office, to quote Brenda's words—'is a doll-faced, over-painted, under-dressed flirt, who hasn't a clue. Mr Bennett turns brick-red to the point of apoplexy at least twice a day, and I can't see how she'll last!'

Tony's card was brief and to the point. Exams had begun, he was studying hard, and she was not to worry if he didn't write for a few weeks.

While Marisa did her shopping in Mareeba the next day, Cesare checked into the hospital and had the plaster removed from his ankle. It was a relief when the X-ray proved satisfactory, for she hesitated to think what he would have been like if the ankle had had to be re-set. Heaven forbid, it didn't bear thinking about!

The following evening brought Tania's engagement party in the Mareeba Shire Hall. Marisa chose to wear a sleeveless dress of jade green crimplene, its circular skirt falling in soft folds from a fitted waist. It was a dress which relied on its colour and simplicity of style, and she instinctively felt it was the right choice. Her hair, freshly washed under the shower just an hour before, fell down her back to her shoulder-blades in a glorious waving flow of shining softness.

Cesare was waiting in the lounge as she left her room, and she felt the quick rush of colour flood her cheeks as he stood with studied ease and let his dark eyes sweep her from head to toe in gentle teasing admiration.

'I hope I'm the one you wish to impress,' he professed lightly, a smile tugging the corners of his generous mouth. He sniffed appreciably as the fragrance of perfume assailed his nostrils. 'Mmmn, that's very delectable,' he complimented.

Marisa made an agitated play of checking her watch, and intimated rather hesitantly that as it was almost eight-fifteen, perhaps they should leave?

'There's plenty of time. Would you like a drink before we go?' he queried, and moved to the cocktail cabinet to pour a small brandy.

She shook her head slowly. 'No, not for me, thank you.' Her eyes widened as he moved towards her. 'I mean—we'll be drinking at the party——' she faltered, unsure of him in this assumed pose of teasing indolence.

His dark gaze fastened on hers, and she lowered her eyes almost immediately.

'Still shy of me, after four—or is it five weeks of marriage?' he queried gently. 'My dear girl, you mustn't scuttle backwards every time I move towards you,' he chuckled softly in amusement, 'or it will be thought I beat you.'

Her thick darkly fringed lashes swept upwards in surprise, which quickly turned to confusion as he caught her face between his hands and lowered his head. His lips were warm against hers, moving with a bewitching sensuality as she gave a half-frightened murmur of protest and placed her hands against his chest. His lips increased their pressure, and his arms enfolded her against the hard length of him. She choked back an unuttered sob, her hands reaching up, clutching the broad expanse of his shoulders as the relentless pressure of his mouth continued.

Slowly, at last, his hold slackened, and as he straightened he drew a teasing finger down her jaw and traced her lips gently, feeling them quiver slightly beneath his touch.

'Enchanting,' he said softly, delighting in her bewilderment. 'You work very hard at being a dutiful wife, *carina*. You have,' he intoned deeply, allowing his gaze to rove intimately over the contours of her face, 'the willing heart,' he finished quietly, lightly flicking her retroussé nose. He smiled indulgently as he picked up the discarded tumbler of brandy and downed its contents in one gulp.

Marisa watched his movements with fascination, unable to tear her eyes away from that strong tanned throat beneath the proud head thrust back, and the large broad hand that held the tumbler. She felt overwhelmed, and a little hurt that he should choose to play with her, to use her inexperience in idle amusement. Could she help it that while her friends had gone out on dates, she had stayed at home in an effort to console her father just by being there for him to talk to, and then later to watch over him and patiently attempt to explain away the grave symptoms of his illness? And there had always been Tony.

She blinked rapidly, and stepped quickly through to the dining-room to collect Tania's gaily wrapped gift from the table, and heard Cesare take the tumbler to the kitchen accompanied by a dull chink as it was placed on the bench. She clutched the parcel against her as he switched off lights, made fast the door, and followed her to the car.

The party was under way with a large collection of guests, all smiling and laughing when she entered the brightly lit Hall with Cesare. Mr and Mrs Petricevic stood together with Tania and Nick welcoming and ready to introduce their intended son-in-law as the guests arrived.

Tania looked fabulous in her gold crêpe dress, appearing intensely bright and very eager to show off the magnificent cluster of diamonds on the third finger of her left hand. She greeted Marisa effusively, affectionately hugging her, before turning to the man by her side.

Nick Bragovic was dark, and quite good-looking in rather a rugged way, Marisa thought, instantly liking him as she shook his hand. He was five, perhaps six inches taller than Tania, and bore the sophisticated air of a successful businessman. He was quite, but one look into those eyes and she very much doubted whether Tania would have everything her own way.

Introductions over, Marisa moved further into the

Hall, conscious of Cesare's hand at her elbow as he led her towards a group of friends.

Tania gave every appearance of being gay and happy throughout the evening, and certainly smiled at everyone ecstatically, while Nick was there at her side looking perfectly at ease as he talked with various guests.

'I meant to tell you,' Cesare began, leaning down a little so she could hear above the noise, 'Tony's college finishes up on December the sixth, and he's booked on the afternoon flight from Brisbane. It arrives in Cairns just after eight. I've written to say we'll meet him.'

He watched as she turned her face towards him, and saw the wealth of happiness revealed in her eyes at his words.

'Oh, Cesare, how marvellous! Is he to stay for the whole of the holidays?' she questioned him eagerly.

He shook his head slowly, and drained the contents of his glass before answering. 'I've given permission for him to attend a camp, Outback, with the rest of his class, but he'll be here almost a month.'

Marisa hardly heard his words as she did quick mental calculations. Three weeks, Tony would be here in just under three weeks!

'Now, perhaps we can attempt to dance for a while, hmm?' he suggested quietly, leading her among the dancing couples.

She felt at a loss held in his arms, for he was so tall and broad, it was like dancing with a Goliath. Her nose was level with the breast-pocket of his jacket, and close to him like this she could smell the pungent woodsy fragrance of his particular brand of aftershave. She began to feel quite cross with herself that she should feel weak at the knees and rather bemused generally. Drat the man, that she should be so vulnerable and unsophisticated! What would he do, she conjectured if she were to move closer into the circle of his arms? Look indulgently amused, most probably. It must be patently obvious she was as green as grass.

'You're very quiet.' He leant down, his lips not far from her ear. 'Tired?'

Startled, she lifted her head and found herself looking straight into his eyes. With an effort she forced herself to hold his gaze, and even managed a smile as she shook her head.

'Nevertheless, it's time we left. Come,' he gestured as he stopped rather abruptly, and with his arm round her waist, they weaved their way towards Tania and Nick, who were standing with Mr and Mrs Petricevic at the end of the Hall farewelling departing guests.

Marisa smiled and said how much she had enjoyed the evening, which she had, even if she had devoted some of the time to analysing her muddled emotions.

The cool of the night air enveloped them as they wandered to the car, and by the time they were halfway home Marisa was feeling pleasantly drowsy. She murmured a sleepy goodnight from the lounge as Cesare locked the kitchen door, and wandered tiredly towards her room.

The remaining two and a half weeks to Tony's arrival sped quickly, with nearly all of her waking hours devoted to chores, the cooking and stringing-up tobacco.

Four extra men were engaged towards the end of November, and there was now a total of eight men, plus Cesare and herself, to cook for. Stringing flat out every spare moment she had, and coping with the huge meals and smokos, left no time to think very much about anything, and the only social highlight during those few weeks was midweek after Tania's engagement party, when Cesare invited Tania and Nick as well as the Petricevic family for an informal get-together. Even that ended—began would be more correct—with the menfolk sitting round the dining-room table playing cards and well fortified with wine, while the women sipped coffee as they watched television and chatted.

In nearly all respects she felt she had settled well to her new way of life. She had acquired a routine which worked well, and the meals were not the worry they had first been. Cesare himself was beginning to fill her thoughts, and as each day passed she found herself growing more and more aware of him. At times she would cast him a surreptitious glance, and find he was regarding her enigmatically. The moments when they were alone together were very rare, as he came into the kitchen, and left, with the workers. In the evenings he invariably spent three to four hours in the bulking shed with Carlo, tending and sorting the cured tobacco, and Marisa, weary after spending the best part of sixteen to seventeen hours on the run between kitchen and string shed, would indulge in a warm shower and be fast asleep in her bed by the time Cesare came into the house.

Tania was conspicuous by her absence, for now that Nick had returned to Melbourne, she was busy stringing tobacco for her father and Ivan. The Petricevic family wanted the picking over and done with by Christmas, if possible, so the women could devote their time to all the planning that was involved in getting Tania married.

So it seemed almost before Marisa could turn around, it was the sixth of December and Tony was due for the holidays. She was looking forward tremendously to seeing him again, to actually be able to talk to him and see for herself that he was well and as happy as he said he was in his letters.

In Cairns there were ten minutes to spare before his flight arrived, and she couldn't settle to sit down with the ease Cesare assumed and leaf through magazines. At last the whine of the jet's engines reached her ears, and it seemed only minutes before Tony was there beside her, a cheeky grin on his face as he suffered her ecstatic greeting.

'Hi there!' He hugged her enthusiastically, and turned towards Cesare, grasping his hand.

'Oh, Tony, it's great to see you!' Her voice sounded a little pathetic even to his undiscerning ear, and he looked at her more closely as they moved out of the reception lounge to the car park.

'Hey, what's up?' he questioned as he slung his bags into the boot of the car.

'Why, nothing,' she looked startled, and then reassured him, 'everything's fine. We're just so busy, that's all. How's college?' she hastily changed the subject as she slid in beside Cesare.

Tony slipped through into the back seat and leant forward as Cesare set the car in motion.

'Terrific! I'm beginning to pick up the threads of it again, it's amazing how much you can forget in the space of a year. I've brought a few of my books to study up over the break, but if you're flat stick, I'd like to help out.'

Marisa half-turned in the front seat and smiled impishly. 'Well, it would be a terrific help if you could take over feeding all the poultry—and incidentally, killing and cleaning them for me,' she began, wrinkling her nose expressively. 'And, if you do ever feel domestically inclined, there's always a gargantuan pile of dishes to get rid of after every meal.'

Cesare chuckled as Tony said, 'The poultry, yes—as to the dishes, sorry and all that, but no.'

Marisa grinned, and made a face at him. 'Piker!'

'I don't know much about tobacco, but perhaps I could help out in the paddock?' Tony suggested to Cesare, who replied urbanely that he was sure they could find something for him to do.

Incredibly, it seemed only a short while before they turned off the main road for the crunchy gravel and dirt track leading to the farm, and Marisa's heart swelled with pride as she anticipated Tony's reaction to Cesare's home. The car swung into the yard, halting under the verandah, and Cesare indicated that they should go into the house as he wanted to check some details with Carlo and would join them shortly.

Tony nodded, and hefted his bags from the boot of the car, following his sister into the house.

She marvelled that in a sense it was *her* home, too, and knowing Tony would be impressed gave her pleasure.

'Wowee!' he whistled appreciatively. 'I take it this *is* the family residence?'

'Yes,' she acquiesced modestly. 'It's nice, isn't it?'

'You can say that again. Nice is a punitive definitive!' He glanced round the dining-room, the large well-equipped modern kitchen, and the comfortable luxury of the spacious lounge.

'I'll take you through to your room first, so that you can get rid of your bags, and then I'll make some coffee.'

She led him through to the spare fourth bedroom, and he put his bags on the floor.

'Come on, I'll show you over the rest of the house,' she grinned at him, taking him on a tour of inspection. She decided rather doubtfully to tell him she and Cesare had separate rooms, for he would find out in the very near future, and rather than risk him making any comment in Cesare's company, she deemed it wiser for him to know now, while she had him on his own.

'You've got to be kidding?' he gaped, openly amazed.

Colour suffused her cheeks as she sought to explain. 'Actually, I'm not. We—agreed to allow ourselves time to get to know one another better. After all,' she continued desperately, 'there were only a few days in between when we met, and were married,' she finished up, by way of explanation.

'Yeah, but hell——' he began, and she interrupted firmly.

'Please, Tony, I don't want to discuss it. Come on, you can unpack later.'

She made for the kitchen, setting the percolator on to heat, and took some cake and biscuits from their tins and set them out on a plate.

'You like him, don't you?' she asked Tony, although it was a statement, more than a question, and he looked surprised.

'Of course, don't you?'

'Well, yes, of course I do,' she answered immediately, startled to think Tony might surmise otherwise.

'Well, then?' he queried, and she sighed with exasperation.

'Oh, Tony, give over, please!'

'What?' he threw up his hands in the air, and turning, took a piece of cake from the plate. 'You're too much of a prude, do you know that? Heavens alive, girl, you should have lived in the Quaker era, you'd have fitted in well!' He munched the cake, and reached for another piece, taking not the slightest notice of the glare she was directing at him.

'Why can't you accept sex as a necessary physical function, without having to tie it in with love and grand passion? It wouldn't hurt you to sleep with him, after all he's done. It's not even immoral—he's your husband!'

She put her hands to her ears, trying to shut out the words. 'Stop it! For heaven's sake, leave me alone!' She shook her head vehemently as she implored him. 'It's none of your business. None of it!'

The percolator bubbled, and she automatically turned the element control down.

'Women!' Tony stamped out of the kitchen angrily, letting the screen-door slam behind him.

Marisa stood in the kitchen breathing deeply, a sick feeling in the pit of her stomach as self-pity welled up inside her. The continual tension and awareness that Cesare must soon demand that their marriage become a normal one caught up with her, and with a deep convulsive sob she stood clutching the sink-bench, hardly seeing anything through a blur of tears.

She didn't hear footsteps coming up the steps, nor the screen-door click shut. She moved blindly towards the privacy of her room, and ran straight into the hard bulk of a human frame.

'Hey,' Cesare's voice laughingly cautioned above her head, 'steady on!' His hands grasped her shoulders, and, alarmed that he might see her tears, she kept her head downbent.

'Marisa? Is anything wrong?' he queried, frowning, unable to see her face for the curtain of hair falling forward. She looked down at her shaking hands and shook her head, trying half-heartedly to escape his hold.

With firm strong fingers that permitted no resistance, he took her chin and lifted her face. Marisa clutched at his hands in desperation, but her efforts were futile.

'*Dio Madonna!*' he expostulated grimly, seeing the tears coursing down her cheeks. 'What has upset you?' he questioned relentlessly, his expression becoming hard and implacable as she tried to avoid those glittering dark eyes boring down, raking the contours of her face ruthlessly.

'Marisa?' he commanded, his voice deceptively quiet as he demanded an answer.

'I—it's my head,' she stammered despairingly, 'The excitement—seeing Tony, the drive down the Range, and—back again,' she stumbled over the words, desperately trying to make them sound feasible.

Cesare released his grip on her chin, and slid a hand round to grasp the back of her head. She winced as his fingers caught in her hair.

'No, *nina*. That I do not believe. Tony, what did he say?'

She looked up at him wordlessly, catching her breath as he moved his fingers through her hair.

'You are so afraid of me?' he queried quietly, easing his thumb down each cheek in turn, gently erasing her tears.

Not quite sure, Marisa hesitantly shook her head.

'Perhaps it is for Tony you are afraid? If you do not tell me, little one, I shall demand of him an explanation,' he assured inflexibly, dangerously formidable as he towered over her.

He would too, she thought ruefully. And Tony, being Tony, wouldn't hesitate to tell him.

'When—when I showed Tony through the house,' she began timidly, 'he—I thought it best to tell him we have separate rooms,' she finished miserably.

'I see,' he began with deceptive mildness. 'And *that* upset you?' His eyes glittered, *smouldered* down at her, and she swallowed convulsively.

'Oh, please,' she implored brokenly, 'don't—don't get so—angry. I can't seem to think straight any more,' she faltered, rubbing a hand childishly across her forehead. 'I'm so mixed up. You—you play cat-and-mouse games with me,' she ventured, rushing on where angels might have feared to tread. 'You do,' she haltingly continued. 'I keep—waiting for you to p-pounce,' she finished, her voice quivering with pent-up emotion.

He allowed his eyes to dwell on the stricken face he held tilted upward for several long seconds, then Marisa saw the ghost of a smile tug the corners of his mouth.

'I'm not sure I approve your comparison, Marisa,' he said gently, releasing his hold on the back of her head. 'Do not frown, little one,' he softly flicked her cheek, then placed a finger beneath her chin. 'I shall endeavour not to pounce, at least not yet.'

She blushed a little at the wryness of his tone, and twisted her hands together nervously.

'You must think me very foolish, and—ridiculously naïve,' she began, her eyes fixed on the shirt button directly in front of her.

'No, *carina.* Just very shy, and in need of reassurance. Now, do you feel better? That coffee has just about bubbled itself away,' he commented, reaching into his pocket for cigarettes and matches.

'Oh, heavens!' she flew to the percolator and lifted it off the element, pouring the contents down the sink. She set about making fresh coffee, and was on the point of pouring it into cups when Tony re-entered the dining-room. He greeted Cesare amicably, shot a searching glance in Marisa's direction, and launched into a witty account of the unfortunate outcome of one of his teacher's lectures. It was almost midnight when she excused herself and went to bed, pleasantly weary, and relieved in more ways than one that Cesare and Tony seemed on friendly terms.

CHAPTER ELEVEN

TONY fitted into farm life with ease. He rose early each morning and went into the paddock with the workers, putting in the long hours that Cesare and the others did.

The weather was hot, so hot that most brows were covered in sweat from early morning right through to early evening. The wet season was almost upon them, and soon it would rain heavily, all day, for days on end. The air was oppressive, even the poultry seemed limp and listless as they wandered aimlessly in search of a cool spot to rest.

Gift shopping for Christmas was a very hurried affair, and as Cesare seemed to have everything, it was very difficult to decide what to buy. After much deliberation, she finally selected a cigarette case and had it gift-wrapped. For Tony, she chose a Parker pen and pencil set, and purchased a gift-box of toiletries for Rosa in appreciation of all the help she had given during those first few weeks.

As Christmas Day drew nearer, Cesare and Carlo were both desperately trying to organise the workers to ensure that there was no picking that day, and to achieve this three barns were picked the preceding day. 'Ai-aye-ai!' breathed in Marisa, slowly in a long-drawn-out sigh, as at nine o'clock in the evening she and Rosa, along with Tony, Cesare and Carlo, were still stringing tobacco under the verandah.

Christmas morning dawned and seemed like any other morning, for the men helped Cesare and Carlo in the bulking shed for a few hours until lunch-time when they finished up for the day. After making for the showers, and in a fresh change of clothes, they filed into the dining-room to sit with their usual waiting expectancy. The only difference Marisa noticed was that they ate with more relish than usual, and were more convivial. No one seemed to notice she wore a new dress and had applied make-up with care, or that her hair was upswept in a style that had taken over half an hour to effect. Even Tony, her own brother, seemed immersed in the men's conversation and scarcely afforded her a second glance. And if Cesare did notice her appearance, he gave no outward sign.

Beer and wine flowed very freely, and inevitably she was left with a table full of dirty dishes and a sink overflowing with saucepans. Everywhere she turned there seemed to be an empty beer bottle, and she felt the tears prick her eyes. So far not even Tony had wished her a Merry Christmas. She clenched her hands, and shut her eyes tightly, determined not to cry. Decidedly the best plan was to work it off, and three quarters of an hour later the dishes were done and stacked away, the floor swept and washed over with the wet-mop, and the empty bottles all stacked in cartons and deposited in the laundry.

The evening meal was to be a joint effort by both Rosa and herself, and eaten on trestles set up under the verandah between the barns and the bulking shed, and both families plus all the workers were to sit down together to a feast of food and drink.

Marisa was slicing onions on the chopping board when she heard a tap at the door. She swung round to see Rosa in the dining-room, a cheerful smile on her face.

'I just called to see how you are managing.'

Marisa grinned companionably, and indicated the pile of potatoes waiting to be roasted. 'What do you think, is that enough? I'm sure there's enough there for an army!'

Rosa chuckled. '*Si, si,* but these men, they eat plenty. Better to have too many than not enough!' She quickly estimated the quantity, and nodded. 'Oh, *si,* Marisa, that should do okay. I have everything ready, and the kids, they drive me *nuts*!' She threw her hands up in the air in a gesture that indicated that maybe someone up there might send her patience. 'When does Papa Natale come, that is all they can ask! When I tell them, "after dinner", they cry it is too long to wait. *Dio mio,* I am so glad when today is over!'

Marisa dissolved into laughter, and there were tears

in her eyes. 'Oh, Rosa, you know you wouldn't have it any other way! Come on, we'll have some coffee, just as soon as I finish these,' indicating the onions.

A few minutes later she collected two cups and saucers, and set the percolator to simmer, and when she would have added some cake and biscuits on a plate, Rosa waved her hands in a gesture of restraint.

'No, no, already I have eaten too much, and to-night——' she shrugged, and shook her head in resignation. 'I am very glad when the season it is over. I shall enjoy, just to sit down. Not to do anything, you understand, when I sit down. We all go, Carlo, myself and the kids, to Port Douglas during school holidays, in May, for two, maybe three weeks. Cesare say we can have the cottage there,' Rosa enlightened, with a huge smile. 'Ah, *mamma mia*,' she sighed prodigiously, 'to sit in the sun, on the beach, while Carlo he go fishing every day!'

Marisa poured the coffee and brought it to the dining-room table.

'When does the picking finish, Rosa?' she queried with interest as she spooned sugar into her cup and stirred it round.

'Two, maybe three more weeks, it depends. Then we grade, but it is better then, no early morning coffee, only breakfast for the men, and no morning smokos. Three, maybe four men finish up when the picking it is over, and me, I do not even grade. The hard work for the women, it is soon finished now.'

Rosa sipped her coffee with enjoyment, and Marisa pondered her age. Teresa, her eldest daughter, was ten years old, so it was reasonable to assume she was in her early thirties.

'The first sale is early this year,' Rosa continued, chatting companionably. 'It will be good, I hope. The buyers, who knows what the buyers will do? Some years, they buy everything and the price it is good, very good, and the next year they fussy, no this, no that, and the price——' Rosa shook her head mournfully. 'For the farmer it is always all right, but for the share-farmer to get not too good price it is very bad,' she shrugged, shaking her head, then drained her cup and stood to her feet, intimating the need to chide the men into setting up the trestles under the verandah.

Marisa was almost ready when the screen-door banged and both Cesare and Tony appeared, to begin carrying out the plates of food.

Roberto, Rosa's son, scurried into the kitchen all spruce in his good clothes, and excitedly stated that Mama was ready, was Marisa?

Cesare repeated the request in louder tones, and she answered from her bedroom that she almost was, and would be there in a few minutes.

With butterflies fluttering wildly in her stomach, she entered the kitchen, and was rewarded with a stunned silence from both men. Her hair had been tidied and coaxed into its former style of several hours previously and her dress had been selected with care, the rich apricot hues serving to heighten her fair complexion.

Tony was the first to comment, by way of a drawn-out whistle of appreciation, and Cesare's raised eyebrows and quizzical expression set her heartbeats hammering.

To cover her confusion she quickly picked up the remaining two serving dishes and followed the men down the steps towards the verandah. Rosa smiled at her as the men sat down, the children having got to their seats at least ten minutes before, and after a few words from Cesare, everyone began to help themselves.

Gradually the food diminished, along with copious quantities of beer and wine, and there was much laughter and story-telling by the men. At one stage all eyes were upon her, with many of the men chuckling between themselves, and at her bewilderment, Rosa leant over and confided quietly:

'They are saying that the next time they sit down to such a feast, it will be for the christening of your first child.'

Marisa smiled in hesitant confusion, and to her chagrin felt a blush steal over her cheeks. She dared not look at Cesare, and picked at the rest of her food, her appetite gone.

The men, at last fully replete, formed two teams to play darts, and insisted that Rosa join Carlo's team and Marisa Cesare's. The result was rather hilarious as Marisa was a beginner at the game and Rosa was not a great deal better. There was much rivalry between the two teams. Beer and wine continued to flow, although the men seemed little affected by the quantity they consumed, and the record-player loudly emitted Italian melodies which by almost midnight had most of the men boisterously joining in.

It seemed hours before the workers wandered off to bed, and she could begin with Rosa to collect glasses while Cesare, Carlo and Tony stacked empty wine flagons and beer bottles into cartons.

'*Buona notte,*' Cesare saluted as Rosa and Carlo disappeared into the surrounding darkness of the yard. Casually he slipped an arm about Marisa's shoulders, drawing her close in to his side as he switched out the verandah lights. Of Tony there was no sign, and Marisa pondered if he had purposely gone into the house ahead of them so she and Cesare would be alone together.

They strolled the few hundred feet beween the verandah to the house in companionable silence. There was no moon to cast a pale glow on the fresh night air, and darkness seemed to enfold them. Marisa viewed the dim shape of the house as it loomed before them, and as they climbed the steps could not account for the sudden shambolic upsurge of nervous tension which began to cause havoc with her breathing.

The screen-door clicked shut behind them as Cesare secured the catch and closed the back door. Marisa sought to escape the arm that still held her without appearing anxious to do so, but Cesare had no intention of letting her go so easily.

'Oh no, little one, you do not escape me. Come,' he said quietly, leading her into the lounge.

He took a small package from his pocket and handed it to her. '*Buon natale, carina,*' he said with a slow smile, his eyes softening as she showed a childish delight in undoing the wrapping.

'Oh, Cesare!' she breathed hesitantly, overwhelmed by the exquisite medallion and its delicately linked chain of gold. 'It's beautiful!' She looked up at him shyly, intensely aware of him standing so close, only inches away. 'Thank you,' she said sincerely. 'I've something for you, too. It's in my room, I'll just get it,' she finished quickly, and escaped to collect the gift she had left nestling beneath her pillow.

In the lounge, she solemnly handed it to him and wished him a 'Happy Christmas', watching anxiously as he undid the box.

'Thank you, Marisa,' he voiced affably. 'I shall use it as often as is practical.' He smiled gently down at her, and caught her shoulders with his hands.

'Goodnight, *nina*,' he said quietly, bending his head down to hers as his lips sought the soft sweet mouth quivering tremulously. Her mouth parted in protest as his lips hardened demanding and, panic-stricken, she pushed futilely against the hard muscles of his chest. Her impulse to struggle was effectively stilled as his arms imprisoned her inescapably against him.

Oh, God, a tiny voice whispered inside of her, as his passion caught her like a swimmer suddenly stricken with cramp in a deep and turbulent sea. She clung desperately on to his shoulders in the need to grasp hold of something *real,* as her senses reeled and soared heavenward. Of their own volition her hands crept to his neck, her fingers entwining themselves in the thick curling hair. Time had no meaning, and when at last he loosened his hold and lifted his head, Marisa looked dazedly up at him, her hands shaking uncontrollably as she pressed them to her burning cheeks.

Cesare swore softly and cupped her face gently between his hands. 'Do not look at me as if I were the Devil himself, *mia*,' he said steadily. 'Would you deny me a kiss on Christmas Day?' There was the suspicion of an indulgent smile at the edge of his mouth as he gazed keenly down at her.

A kiss? He called that ... a *kiss*? She was numb at the depth of her own emotion, and somewhat afraid of herself because of it. Her heart thudded wildly against her ribs and her limbs seemed weak and incapable of any movement at all.

'Bed. Your bed, *nina,*' he said firmly, his warm lips caressing hers. He traced a line slowly along the edge of her jaw with a stray finger, and as a flood of rosy colour swept her cheeks, he said gently, 'I want very much to make love to you, *carina.* It can be a wondrous thing that lovers share. Tonight, you are tired and a little confused, and very much aware of Tony in his room not far away. So,' he straightened and let his hands fall to his sides, turning away from her, 'go quickly, *now,* before my good intentions leave me.'

Marisa hesitated no more than a brief second before escaping to her room, and once there leant against the closed door feeling as breathless as if she had run a mile.

New Year's Eve was celebrated in the customary manner with a large party at a neighbouring farm. It was strictly a bring-your-own food and drink party, and from the number of people present, Marisa wondered if the whole farming community were there. She saw Tania with her mother and father, and smiled through the crowd. It seemed weeks since they had last seen each other.

Tania waved back, and after indicating to her mother where she was going and to whom, she began weaving her way towards Marisa.

'Hi,' she breathed, reaching Marisa's side. 'Long time, no see. How are you?'

Marisa's face creased into a wide smile of welcome. 'Long time, no see, is right! I haven't even seen you at the pictures on a Saturday night.'

Tania grimaced wryly. 'There's to be a wedding, my dear,' she intoned virtuously, imitating her mother, 'it's getting close to the time when the last and youngest of the Petricevic chicks must leave the family nest. Any *spare* time I do get is spent sewing, and *all* the time I am being lectured, if not by my mother, it's Luisa or Anna or Gianna, even Elena. I could utter oaths so terrible,' she indicated darkly with a flash from her dark eyes, 'the saints themselves would quail. I doubt if I can stand it for the next eight weeks!'

'Try wearing ear-muffs, or better still, put cotton wool in your ears,' suggested Marisa with a grin.

'Where's Cesare disappeared to?' Tania queried with a slight smile, and twisted her head this way and that until she spotted him at the far end of the verandah, playing darts.

'God, aren't men the limit! If Nick ever tries to shelve me at a party, I'll scream, really I will,' she vowed with a vengeance. 'Look at them all, the whole darned lot of them! Not a care in the world that their wives might need or want another drink. Oh no,' Tania shook her head emphatically, 'I'll not be the mat beneath Nick's feet, I can assure you!'

Marisa silently thought marital war might be declared soon after Tania's nuptial vows. Nick seemed an inflexible type of man, even autocratic, and Tania was the antithesis of docility.

'Oh dear,' muttered Tania ruefully. 'My mama is getting her feathers ruffled, and is heading this way. Anyone would think, from the way that woman guards me, that some man is waiting to snatch me away to places unknown with intent to commit unmentionable deeds! She loses sight of me for one minute, and hey presto! the worry vibes begin emanating in all directions!'

Marisa caught sight of Cesare looming towards her from the direction of the bar, and both he and Mrs Petricevic arrived almost simultaneously.

'It's almost midnight, have you each got drinks?' Cesare questioned with a wide smile, proceeding there and then to refill their glasses from the flagon of wine he held.

'Hooray!' a tumultuous cry echoed far and wide as the radio blared out midnight chimes. As the last chime sounded, a roar went up that almost shook the rafters supporting the verandah, and everyone kissed their kin, and shook hands with those who weren't.

Cesare took Marisa's hand in his, as most everyone began singing 'Auld Lang Syne' in Italian. Marisa stifled a grin and wondered what a Scotsman would make of it.

Tony appeared beside her and planted a resounding kiss on her cheek. 'Happy New Year, Sis, and God bless,' he wished softly, close to her ear, and she turned to him with tears in her eyes, almost.

'Hey, don't cry, you silly goose, it's New Year,' he protested with a laugh, a rather puzzled frown creasing his face.

How could she tell him the wonderful wholeheartedness of these people, their faith in themselves and their sheer will to succeed in a country not their own had gripped her with overwhelming esteem? That she had glimpsed fleetingly into the years ahead and envisaged the sons she would bear standing tall and proud like their father, working the land at his side.

Cesare drew her firmly into his arms as the record-player emitted the strains of a waltz. It seemed amazing that all the men were dancing with their wives or girlfriends, not one person could she see not dancing. Even Tony had found a girl close by, and was leading her slowly through the mingling crowd.

A wonderful feeling of peace and well-being flowed through her veins, relaxing her completely, and as she felt Cesare's lips on her hair she rested her head against his broad chest.

'Tired?' his voice enquired softly, his hold tightening fractionally. Marisa pondered the question and shook her head, mumbling into his chest. He bent his head lower to catch her words.

'Not tired enough to sleep, but too tired to dance more vigorously than this.'

He smiled, and it was a rare sweet smile which lit up his eyes and softened the rough-hewn face barely inches away.

'Poor *nina*. If your head were to touch a pillow now, your eyes would close within seconds.'

He was right, she mused, not wishing to move away from the closeness of his arms. In fact, she felt so comfortable and secure, she could have closed her eyes right there and then.

As the record changed tempo he gently disentangled her arms from about his waist. '*Andiamo a casa,* I think, little one,' he said quietly. 'We pick tomorrow—today, at least—and if I am not mistaken the rain will soon fall.'

He managed to catch Tony's eye at last, and beckoned that they were leaving.

She remembered watching the road beneath the headlights for what seemed several hundred yards, and then gave up trying to keep her eyes open. She was drowsily conscious of moving slightly, seeking a more comfortable position, but too tired to worry about it, just so long as she could sleep.

A hand shook her shoulder, and she sleepily pleaded to be left alone.

'Marisa, come on, it's nearly seven,' Cesare's deep voice penetrated at last.

She groaned and sat up, rubbing her eyes. 'I don't even remember getting into bed, I was so tired,' she yawned, her eyes widening in consternation as comprehension slowly dawned and she became aware that she was still partly clothed.

He idly watched the blush steal delicately over her face as she endeavoured to look anywhere but directly at him. He bent down, tweaking her cheek in amusement, chiding her to hurry and get up or the men would be in for breakfast before it was ready. And that, she thought wryly, would never do.

As Cesare predicted, the rain began falling a few days later, and Marisa likened it to the heavens literally opening their flood gates. It rained and it rained, the dry red earth sucking in the life-giving water until it became saturated. The rivers that had been mere apologies of creeks rose steadily, swelling into swirling muddy torrents. The poultry sought the shelter of their pen-houses, and perched comfortably as they regarded the teeming sheets of water falling all around them. After a few days Marisa began to wonder if the rain would ever cease.

At the end of the week four men were paid off, and

Tony was due back at college within the next few days. He had changed a lot, and even during the month he had spent on the farm he had matured considerably. He was no longer a tempestuous teenager, up in arms over the wrongs of the world. Cesare's influence had quietened him down remarkably, of this there was no doubt.

On the second Monday in January they drove down to Cairns to the airport to enable Tony to catch the flight to Brisbane. As the plane ascended into the wide blue yonder, Marisa sighed deeply.

'He will return often at vacation time,' Cesare reminded her with a slight smile. 'He is not going to disappear, never to be seen again.'

She looked up at him with a serious expression on her face. 'He's changed so much, grown up somehow,' she enlarged, frowning slightly as they walked across the tarmac to the car.

'But of course, what do you expect?' he asked, unlocking the car to slide in behind the wheel, before leaning across to unlock her door.

'He's like a young puppy who has discovered there's more to life than chasing his tail round in circles.'

Cesare manoeuvred the car out on to the main road and drove towards town. 'I have some business to attend to, it won't take long, then we shall have a quiet drink before heading for home.'

Marisa felt an anticipatory thrill at being able to windowshop for a while, and she slowly browsed among the shops while Cesare attended to whatever it was he considered important.

A pendant caught her eye, and she stood surveying it, her head to one side, trying to make up her mind whether to buy it or not. She felt in a reckless and curiously unsettled mood, and had the urge to spend some money on something luxurious, even frivolous, like an exotic talc, or an expensive perfume. Something.

Inside a chemist's shop, she deliberated with the assistant for several minutes before choosing a gorgeous talc with an exclusive French brand-name, and then impulsively bought perfume to match.

She emerged from the shop feeling extremely guilty. Phew! It was just as well these mad moments didn't happen very often! At that price, perfume was more precious than liquid gold.

She wandered back towards the hotel clutching the precious parcel close to her bosom, and Cesare came out from the bar to meet her with a rather quizzical lift to his eyebrow.

'Why the anxious expression?' he queried with a generous smile. 'You have the look of a wife who has just spent all her husband's money.'

Marisa swallowed and hugged the parcel more closely to her. 'You won't be angry?' she asked hesitantly, and he laughed out loud in genuine amusement.

'Have I reason to be? *Have* you spent all my money?' His dark eyes twinkled down at her as she retrieved his cheque book from her shoulder-bag and handed it back to him. Solemnly he pocketed it without even bothering to look inside, and she shook her head incredulously.

'Aren't you—I mean, don't—doesn't it worry you how much I spent?' she managed at last, her eyes wide.

'It it worries you, then tell me,' he bade her affably as he took her arm, leading her into the lounge and ordering drinks from the hovering waiter.

She sipped her drink, cautiously looking at him over the rim of her glass. He was leaning well back in his chair, and bore the air of a man well satisfied with life.

His eyes gleamed wickedly as he sought to tease her. 'Well, aren't you going to enlighten me as to what you've bought?'

Marisa, shot him a speculative look and grinned ruefully, wrinkling her nose expressively. 'I had one of those madly extravagant impulses we females are prone to, and I'm afraid I spent rather a lot on some new talc, and perfume,' she added hesitantly. 'It's French,' she hastened to explain.

Cesare was having a hard time concealing a hearty

laugh, and his lips twitched as he regarded her across the table.

'Is there any particular reason for this extravagance?'

She shook her head emphatically. There wasn't ... or was there somewhere deep down inside of her an urge to flirt with him a little by using the age-old art of an alluring perfume?

She shook her head again, answering, 'No.' Heavens, she must be weak in the head to entertain the thought of flirting with him. That *would* be playing with fire! As it was, she felt she was walking the proverbial tightrope.

'Come,' he issued urbanely, 'drink your Cinzano. It's time we were leaving.'

As soon as they arrived home Marisa hurried inside to change, for the men would be in to dinner at six, and it would take all her initiative to have the meal on the table by then.

It was almost dark before the kitchen was restored to rights, the meat for the following day extracted from the freezer. There was a good comedy programme on television which she wanted to see, and if Cesare kept to his usual routine of returning from the bulking shed after ten, she would be safely ensconced in her bed.

She tucked her feet up under her on the long cushioned lounge-settee, and comfortably viewed the beginning of one of her favourite programmes. She felt good, and she sniffed appreciatively as the perfume of her new talc wafted off her freshly bathed skin. Mmmn, it was rather gorgeous. The first half-hour held her undivided attention, and then she began to doze a little, slipping down into a more comfortable position so that her head rested against the arm of the lounge-settee. She assured herself she would catnap for ten minutes, see the remainder of the programme, then go to bed.

Hard work, late nights and early mornings, plus the long drive to Cairns and back took their toll, and fresh from a warm soporific shower, Marisa was too tired merely to catnap. She slept soundly, and was unaware an hour later of Cesare entering the house.

As he passed through the lounge, he caught sight of her lying curled up, sleeping as peacefully as a babe, while the television enthralled its viewers with a blood-and-thunder thriller. For a few moments he paused, catching his breath at her defencelessness. Her hair had been pinned neatly back, and in sleep she looked young and very vulnerable.

The steaming hiss of water cascading in the shower-box failed to rouse her, and minutes later Cesare stood regarding her sleeping figure tenderly.

Marisa felt something tickle her cheek and she raised a sleepy hand to brush it off. It was persistent, whatever it was, she thought drowsily, flicking absently at her hair. Then she sat up rather hurriedly, blinking as her eyes focused in the dim light reflected from a distant wall-lamp. *That* was no lock of stray hair, nor was it an idle mosquito. Something had definitely pinched her ear.

'Oh,' she exclaimed with something akin to fright as she saw Cesare's broad frame attired in a dark blue towelling-robe leaning over her. 'You pinched me,' she said accusingly.

'Oh, come now,' he smiled as he sat down beside her, 'it was a fairly gentle pinch.'

She scrambled hurriedly to her feet and almost stumbled in her haste. A long arm shot out and hard fingers gripped her upper arm, steadying her.

'My foot, it's gone to sleep,' she almost wailed as it refused to support her. Firm hands pulled her down on to the lounge-settee and her foot was gently rubbed until the tingling had stopped.

'Thank you,' she said awkwardly, feeling the rush of colour flood her cheeks at the intimate way he was regarding her.

'How much longer, Marisa?' he queried quietly, lifting her chin and turning her face so that she had to look at him or close her eyes. Her stomach muscles contracted nervously, and her colour deepened.

Apprehensively she cleared her throat. 'I—I don't

know what you mean,' her voice was low, so low it was almost a whisper as she gazed desperately into the fathomless dark brown eyes several inches above her own.

There was the suspicion of a smile lurking at the corners of his mouth as he clicked his teeth patiently.

'Marisa, Marisa,' he shook his head imperturbably. 'I can tell from the blush on your cheeks that you understand very well what I mean, hmm? Is that not so, *carina*?' he queried softly, tracing a line down her cheek to her lips and feeling them quiver beneath his touch. 'Such a delightful mouth,' he smiled gently, drawing her closer, his breath warm against her neck as his lips caressed the delicate hollows, biting the shell-like lobes of her ears teasingly before claiming her mouth, tenderly at first, then with a savage ardour which frightened her. Chaotic thoughts born from fear set her struggling against him, yet even as she sought to free herself she was gripped with an unwavering conviction that he meant to share her bed tonight. She wished she could explain her feelings, that perhaps with words she could make him understand that she knew very little of the ways of men, to beg him be patient with her inhibitions.

He stood then and gathered her up against him, kissing her gently before sweeping her into his arms and carrying her into the hitherto unoccupied master bedroom.

In the darkness of the room her heart lurched, hammering hollowly as his arms closed round her. Her lips quivered beneath his as he gently caressed her, and her very being cried out for him to utter words of love, but he did not, and she could have wept, longing for just one word of encouragement.

A few silent tears did trickle their way down her cheeks, long afterwards as she lay listening to his deep rhythmic breathing. Slowly she eased a hand up to smooth back her tumbled hair, and he stirred instantly, gathering her back into his arms. His lips nuzzled into the hollows at her throat, then sought the sweetness of her mouth, detecting the tell-tale dampness on her cheeks as they trailed lingeringly upward.

'Tears, *carina*?' he quizzed gently, and she trembled uncontrollably. His voice, deep and mellifluous, flowed soothingly in reassurance. The words, spoken in Italian, were incomprehensible, although nonetheless comforting, and shortly her eyelids began to droop as sleep gently claimed her.

The bright rays of a new day's dawn streamed warmly through chinks between the gently billowing drapes at the window as Marisa stirred lazily, slowly orientating herself with the strangeness of her surroundings. Of Cesare there was no sign, and all that remained to remind her of their shared intimacy was the imprint of his head on the pillow.

The day passed all too quickly in a whirl of activity equally divided between the kitchen and the stringing up of tobacco under the verandah, but it was a happy day in respect that the last of tobacco was brought in from the paddock, and that, of course, necessitated a celebration drink or two among the men and the remainder of the day off.

At dinner the men were bright and extremely talkative, taking longer than usual to eat their meal, and their mood could only be described as expansive. The pick was over, glory hallelujah! Marisa silently echoed their sentiments, and determined to write to Tony as soon as the kitchen was respectable.

She was in the kitchen setting the percolator on the simmer when the screen-door clicked and Cesare walked into the dining-room. Confusion set her hands trembling as he stood in the aperture between the dining-room and kitchen. She could see him out of the corner of her eyes standing tall and broad, smoke drifting hazily from the cigarette he held in his hand. She spared a swift glance in his direction, speaking hesitantly.

'I'm m-making coffee. Would you like some?'

His voice held a hint of laughter as he affirmed that he would, and he continued on his way through to the bathroom.

He was already sitting in the lounge when she carried the cups through, and she set his down on the coffee table beside his chair, feeling strange and at a loss for words after last night.

'Thanks,' he looked at her quizzically, watching the delicate colour appear on her cheeks. 'I won't bite, you know.' There was amusement in his voice as he caught her hand and pulled her down beside him.

Self-consciously she reached for her coffee and rather desperately plunged into making conversation.

'How is the grading going? Will you finish in time?' she asked in a polite voice, and strove to stir her coffee calmly.

'It will be hard going, but yes, I think we'll make it,' he answered blandly, and had she been looking at him she would have seen the twinkle in his gleaming eyes and the twitch of barely concealed humour at his lips.

Marisa picked up her cup and sipped the hot coffee nervously. 'There are three sales, aren't there? Rosa was telling me the last sale is at the beginning of June, this year,' she commented, and looked everywhere but directly at him. Her hands shook slightly, and she hurriedly replaced the cup on its saucer before the contents spilt. 'Take a deep breath, control yourself,' she urged her brain to direct her body. Oh, bother, she reflected wryly, why couldn't she be more sophisticated or something, and appear normal? Not churned up inside with all her nerve-ends quivering, aching, with an awareness that bewildered her.

'Did you know,' she began, holding her hands together tightly in her lap, 'that Rosa and Carlo are taking the children down to the beach at Port Douglas for a holiday during the May vacation?' She cast him a quick look from beneath her thickly fringed lashes, and put a hand to her hair in a purely nervous gesture, smoothing it back behind her ears. Cesare lifted his hand lazily, catching her fingers as they left her hair, holding them captive in his large hand.

'I—they'll love the beach, and Rosa says they'll spend more time in the water than out of it,' she rushed on, startled by his action. She was aware she was babbling, but it seemed imperative to keep talking.

Cesare extracted a cigarette, and put it between his lips, then returned the same hand to his pocket for matches. When he had exhaled the smoke from the first long draw, he turned to look at her with an inscrutable expression.

'Carlo and I usually take it in turns to have a holiday after the season is over. With luck on our side, we should have all the grading completed by the end of March, then there is the baling, but we'll be able to get away for two, perhaps three weeks towards the end of April, all going well. I thought we might go down to Sydney.'

It sounded lovely, and she said so, a shine in her eyes as she turned to him.

'Oh, Cesare, could we really?' It seemed incredible that suddenly there was a rainbow with a little pot of gold at the end of it.

He nodded, stubbing out his cigarette. 'I thought it would appeal to you. While we were in Cairns yesterday I made a tentative booking through an agency there,' he informed her with a smile. She was like an unspoilt child faced with the prospect of a wonderful treat in store.

'And now, my little goose,' he said gently, standing to his feet and pulling her up beside him, 'it is time for bed, hmm?'

Marisa felt herself blushing delightfully at this suggestion, and lowered her eyes in sudden shyness. Hard-sinewed arms crushed her against the length of him until she could scarcely breathe, and his lips met hers hungrily as if he would draw the very soul from her. She could not deny that he awoke responses she had never dreamed of possessing, and she longed to reach up and clasp that proud head down to hers and whisper words of love. There was no doubt he wanted her, and with an aching heart she yearned to believe it was more than assuaging a physical need.

CHAPTER TWELVE

DAYS became weeks, and as each passed she became achingly aware of her love for Cesare. Determined to adopt an attitude of astute common sense, she resolved not to reach for the moon and hope for too much. It was much more logical to reason that he was *her* husband, and good health prevailing and barring accidents, there were something like forty years ahead of them. Put it like that, she thought with a slight smile, and it sounds *most* optimistic!

The first tobacco sale was a success financially, and the second sale heralded an end to the grading.

Tania and Nick were married on the first Saturday in March, and the wedding was a splendid affair, with the Shire Hall in Mareeba filled to capacity with guests. The entire Yugoslav community were present, and it seemed a vast majority of the Italians were there as well. Tania looked fabulous in her wedding gown, which Marisa noted with a smile was indeed a Victorian style as she had vowed it would be. Nick carried the evening off with commendable aplomb, handling Tania's tears with remarkable ease when it came time to bid everyone farewell. It was understandable that she should weep, everyone murmured among themselves. Why, she was leaving behind all her family and friends, and Melbourne was a considerable distance away. Marisa felt rather sad that she and Tania hadn't seen much of each other since New Year, although they had spoken on the telephone a few times. Tania had confided that she and Nick were to spend their honeymoon at Surfers' Paradise, and Marisa wished time would go quickly, for she was excitedly anticipating her holiday in Sydney. The shops to explore, the nightclubs, and the most wonderful thing of all was Cesare's company. For two to three weeks he would be there all the time, there would be no paddocks or bulking sheds claiming his attention.

She danced a jig all round the kitchen on the day the last two men were paid off, and had the grace to look ashamed when Cesare came in and caught her as she polkaed round and round the kitchen table.

'I'm just so happy there's no more big meals to cook, that it's come to an end for a few months,' she smiled happily up at him. 'I'll have time to catch up on some reading and sewing, and I can just *sit*!' She laughed as he assumed a look of mock indignation.

'Sit? No Italian women *just sit, nina*. They knit or sew, or mend, write letters——'

Marisa interrupted him gaily. 'I know, I know, always industriously occupied. But I warn you, I'm going to devote at least three hours one day to just *sitting* and thinking profound thoughts without any interruptions whatsoever!' She wagged a finger at him playfully, then yelped as he caught a handful of long honey-gold hair and pulled her towards him, bending his head to kiss her hard on the mouth.

He released her a short while later, smiling devilishly down at her soft rosy lips still quivering from his kiss, then bent his head and kissed her again.

'I, too, am glad this season is behind us,' he said ambiguously, reaching into the refrigerator for the carafe of wine. 'We should be able to leave for Sydney next Friday week,' he informed her as he poured some of the dry red wine into a glass. 'Carlo and I will finish baling at the end of this week, then we'll need a day to disc all the stalks in, and there's a few odd things which will need taking care of, but all going well Friday should see us on the plane.'

She turned to him eagerly, her eyes alight with pleasure. 'Can we really, so soon?'

Cesare nodded, tossing back the contents of the glass. 'We'll garage the car in Cairns, and fly down on the early morning flight.'

For the next few days Marisa relaxed, enjoying a freedom from cooking large meals, and revelled in being able to exchange morning coffee with Rosa. She was so happy, she all but skipped about her chores each day.

With a contemplative scrutiny she inspected the walls and ceilings, and decided on a grand-scale spring-cleaning. It would be much better to get it all done before they went away and then she wouldn't have it hanging over her head while they were on holiday. It took four full days, but it was worth it. All the major tasks she had had little time for during the season. Blankets were washed and aired, mattresses turned, curtains washed and ironed, vinyl floor-coverings scrubbed down and repolished, windows cleaned until they sparkled, cupboards turned out and shelves re-lined. She was exhausted when she fell into bed on Thursday night, but exhausted in a happy sort of way, for tomorrow their holiday would begin. Cesare had gone into Mareeba with Carlo for a few drinks at the hotel, and she was so tired she didn't hear the car come up the drive, nor Cesare come into the house.

There was no need for her to be shaken awake next morning, for she was up and dressed at five, preparing coffee and a light breakfast for them both. Their suitcases were packed, and there were only last-minute things to pop into an overnight bag when she went back into the bedroom to call Cesare. He was already up and dressing and as she made the bed she was conscious of his eyes following her every move. She patted the bedspread into place, then yelped when he slapped her none too gently as she bent over the bed.

'Ouch!' she cried reproachfully, 'that hurt!'

A slow wide smile spread over his broad-chiselled features as he reached out and pulled her into his arms. He kissed her gently and tweaked her nose. 'Come, this is no time for dallying,' chuckling at her expression of incredulity.

Driving away from the farm, Marisa looked at the swiftly fleeting scenery and drew a deep breath. The sun in the sky suddenly seemed much brighter than usual, the green leaves of trees and mulgascrub became alive with insect life flitting about its daily life, and the red loamy earth positively glowed in the soft early morning light. At this hour there was a wonderful clean freshness in the air, and she felt like singing with sheer joy.

There were fifteen minutes to spare on their arrival

at the airport in Cairns, and that passed swiftly as their bags were weighed and checked in, tickets allocated their seat numbers and the car keys handed over to the official responsible for garaging it.

Marisa was sufficiently enthralled to watch the plane's ascent with interest before settling back in her seat to leaf through magazines. There was a brief stop-over at Townsville en route to Brisbane where they changed planes for Sydney. She could scarcely contain her excitement and picked at the contents of her lunch-tray with little appetite. It was going to be wonderful to visit the huge department stores and explore the teeming cosmopolitan metropolis.

Cesare hired a car, a large Ford Falcon, and drove to their motel in the suburb of Bondi. In their suite, Marisa gasped at the luxurious, almost opulent furnishings, and felt in awe of her surroundings. Electing to unpack first, she resisted the temptation to leave it until later, and had showered and changed and was pushing the last suitcase under the bed as Cesare shrugged his powerful shoulders into the jacket of his suit.

'Ready?' he queried, and she smiled at him, eager to begin an inspection of the inner city.

'Yes,' she agreed demurely in an effort to hide her excitement.

Her dress was long, in soft autumn tonings of brown, gold and russet on a white background. It was sleeveless with a flatteringly scooped neckline, and the skilfully styled princess line accentuated her slimness, giving her a curiously fragile air.

Cesare drove into the city and parked the car, and it took quite a while to stroll several blocks as Marisa simply could not help windowshopping along the way, exploring several arcades, and all thoughts of food were forgotten until Cesare firmly led her into a licensed restaurant for dinner. The food was wonderful, and he ordered champagne, indulgent when she protested that it always went straight to her head. Marisa watched the entertainment with avid interest, and danced with Cesare, unable to believe the witching hour of midnight was almost upon them.

'Cesare,' she smiled and caught his hand as they entered their motel suite. 'Thank you for being so tolerant with me,' she finished sincerely, then spoilt the effect by hiccupping.

'Oh dear,' she looked faintly shocked, and Cesare burst out laughing.

'You've had one too many, *piccolina,*' he murmured, shaking his head in amusement.

'Well, it's all your fault,' she accused with a smile, shaking a fist at him. 'You poured the wine,' this was said very self-righteously. 'Anyway, it's just my digestive system protesting at the variety of rich food and wine it's had to contend with these last few hours. See?' she held out one hand in front of her and recited—'pretty Polly peeled a peck of pickled peppers,' beautifully. 'I'm slightly inebriated, happily, pleasantly so,' she declared with dignity as he reached out and drew her against him.

'Is that so?' he commented, bending his head to meet her lips with a passionate intensity.

The light was streaming through the venetian blinds at the window next morning when she stirred, and as she lifted her head it thumped dully. She peeped at her watch and groaned, for it was already after ten o'clock. Her head didn't belong to her, and she was sure her stomach had its reservations as well.

'Coffee, I believe, is great for a hangover,' Cesare's voice suggested humorously, and she rolled over to face him.

He smiled down at her and held out a cup on its saucer. 'Come, young lady, sit up and sip this. I promise you will feel more with this world when you do.'

Marisa did so, discreetly pulling the sheet high up over her bosom, which drew a twinkle from Cesare's dark eyes as they rested on her.

Ah, that coffee was indeed good, and she had to admit that she felt a lot better when she had finished it. After a hot shower she felt even better, and with some toast and a second coffee inside her she felt ready to face the day.

They took a ferry to Taronga Park Zoo, arriving

back in the city in time to change leisurely for dinner, and this time Marisa managed to persuade Cesare to try a Chinese restaurant as she adored Chinese cooking. He smiled tolerantly and allowed himself to be led out to the car as she eagerly described some of her favourite oriental dishes, and after an entirely satisfactory meal they wandered about Kings Cross which lived up to her expectations and more! It all seemed like something from the television screen and not quite real.

The days that followed were carefree and wonderful, and Marisa revelled in the shopping spree on which Cesare indulgently led her, and she thought ecstatically that she had never been so happy in her entire life.

On the fifth evening they visited friends of Cesare's in the exclusive suburb of Double Bay. As she coaxed her hair into an upswept style of elaborate swirls, she hoped its sophisticated style lent her a few extra years. It looked becoming, and she was more than pleased as she stood back from the mirror viewing her reflection critically. Yes, she nodded with satisfaction, that should do very well. The long flowing skirt of softly crushed velvet was worn with an identically matched fuchsia halter-necked jersey-silk top, and she gathered up the cream mohair wrap from the bed.

Cesare looked up from reading the paper as she entered the lounge and it seemed several seconds before he rose to his feet, smiling slowly across the room at her.

'You look charming,' he complimented gently, indicating his partly filled glass. 'A drink?'

Marisa shook her head, then changed her mind. 'Yes, perhaps I will, thank you.'

He poured her a small glass of light golden sherry, and she sipped it appreciatively. By the time she had finished, it was beginning to give her the lift she felt she needed to get through the evening. She had to admit that the thought of meeting strange people and having to make light conversation all evening was beginning to make her feel nervous. Not that she was lacking in the art of conversing pleasantly and with ease with strangers, but somehow tonight for some reason it hung heavily on her—so much so that she wished the evening over and done with.

The car swung out into the stream of city-bound traffic, and she marvelled at the skill with which Cesare negotiated the car. Sydney was notorious for its risk-mad, speed-crazy drivers, and she supposed one could get used to it, but was thankful it was not she behind the wheel. The sun had settled down to spread a hazy glow, which, intermingled with a smoky screen over the harbour, lent a lazy air to their surroundings as they sped swiftly towards their destination. Already street lights were springing on all around them, and soon darkness would fall and the city would be a fairyland by night.

The little knot of nerves in Marisa's stomach seemed to grow as Cesare parked the car under the portico framing the magnificent entrance to their host's home.

The door opened as they mounted the few stairs, and a dark-suited grey-haired man stood smiling with both hands extended in welcome.

'Cesare! *Amico*!' he bellowed melodiously, and grasped Cesare's arms before giving his shoulder a hearty slap. Then he turned his attention to Marisa as Cesare introduced her.

'*La mia moglie,* Marisa.' Cesare placed an arm about her shoulders and smiled down at her. 'Marisa, this is an old friend of my father, Ottorino Donati.'

She smiled, murmuring a greeting, and the man's eyes creased deeply as he leant forward and kissed both her cheeks, then stood holding her arms, looking down at her, speaking in Italian to Cesare.

'Come in, come in,' he swept his arm and gestured for them to precede him into the foyer, then led the way to a lounge which almost made Marisa gasp aloud, so exquisitely perfect were the furnishings. It resembled a feature-spread in glamorous colour from *House and Home,* and she suppressed the uncharitable feeling that it was designed more for visual pleasure than comfortable utilisation.

Two women rose from separate chairs, one a gracious matron, and the other a young woman whose age was difficult to determine, for she could have been anything between twenty and thirty. She looked so soignée and ... yes, ultra-sophisticated, she could easily have stepped straight out from a page in *Vogue* magazine. Even her facial expression was carefully contrived to give the impression of an élite aloofness.

'Cesare,' they both spoke simultaneously, moving forward to greet him, and Marisa smiled hesitantly as she was introduced.

Ottorino and Rafaella's daughter, Francesca, gave Marisa a condescending smile that lacked sincerity and returned her attention to Cesare.

'*Caro*,' she said softly, *intimately*, and Marisa didn't need a translator to tell her that *caro* was Italian for darling. 'It's been so long since you last visited. Why,' she laughed on a quiet note of incredulity as she spread her hands, 'we only recently heard you had married.'

Rafaella smiled at Marisa, and said charmingly to Cesare, 'We were delighted to hear at last you had chosen a wife, and we wish you both every happiness.'

Ottorino beamed expansively, adding his felicitations, calling their attention to the champagne he had opened, and proceeded to hand glasses of the sparkling wine to each of them in turn.

Marisa smiled up at Cesare rather doubtfully as she sipped the golden liquid, feeling a little unsure of him in these surroundings and realising how little she really knew of his past. She felt sure in her heart that Francesca *had* been part of his past, and instinct led her to think that as far as Francesca was concerned Cesare had been number one on her list of men friends. What she couldn't understand was why had he chosen *her* when he could obviously have had Francesca. Well, if it came to that, he hadn't chosen her at all ... their marriage had begun as a mutual arrangement of convenience. But it wasn't that now ... was it? *Was it?* 'Not to me,' she cried silently. 'He's my life, my reason, my whole world ... and if he stopped wanting me I would surely die a thousand deaths slowly, one by one, until all of me became an empty aching shell, a nonentity.'

'You're very quiet,' Rafaella commented gently, and Ottorino turned from speaking with Cesare to check her glass.

'Come, my dear, drink up,' he commanded jovially, topping her half-empty glass with more champagne.

'I expect you're pleased the season is over,' Rafaella continued conversationally. 'It can't have been easy for you, cooking for so many, particularly as you haven't been brought up to it. For four months the work is very hard, is it not?'

'Yes, it is,' Marisa answered politely as she sipped her drink.

Musical chimes sounded from the direction of the foyer, and after a brief few seconds a manservant announced that a Signor Agnelli had arrived.

'Marcello!' welcomed Ottorino. 'Come in, my friend.'

A man of average height advanced into the room, apologising as he came for his lateness. He had apparently been held up in traffic, and Marisa brightened a little at the effusive manner with which he greeted Francesca.

Dinner was announced a short while afterwards, and if Marisa thought the lounge exquisite, the dining-room was quite splendid. The long table was decorated with gleaming silverware and delicate porcelain, and glassware of finely cut crystal. The mahogany furniture was burnished to a magnificent gloss and a crystal chandelier hung on a chain from the ceiling.

Marisa's appetite, normally a very healthy one in spite of her slimness, flew out the window as Francesca smiled openly across the table at Cesare, and she had to force herself to do justice to the elaborate meal. With the usual Italian exuberance, her host called for her to eat more, and when she politely refused, Francesca raised her eyebrows and enquired if she had a diet problem. Equally politely Marisa replied that she did not, no, adding that her appetite had disappeared while on holiday. She dared not glance sideways to Cesare at this gross understatement of fact, remembering her shameless justice to the preceding meals since their arrival in Sydney.

Rafaella Donati clucked her tongue and spoke rapidly to Cesare, who, after listening attentively, smiled and replied with equal rapidity.

Francesca eyed Marisa covertly, no doubt preening herself that naturally she understood all that was said, whereas Marisa did not.

Dinner was a leisurely affair, and it was all of ten o'clock when they all left the house, en route to a city nightclub.

If Cesare took notice of Marisa's silence during the drive, he made no comment, in fact he seemed to enjoy the quietness.

Ottorino and Rafaella were waiting for them as Cesare parked the car, and almost immediately Francesca and Marcello joined them.

Marisa was looking forward to being able to dance, and besides, it was her first visit to a nightclub. She was not to be disappointed, for it was an exclusive club, and a floor-show was in progress as they were escorted to their table. Marisa swallowed and sought to conceal her blushes as the female guest singer delivered what must surely have been the sexiest rendition on record, barring Eartha Kitt, of two sultry numbers before finishing with 'Bridge Over Troubled Water'.

As the band played, Cesare indicated that Marisa should dance with him, and they were soon followed on to the floor by Francesca and Marcello. She longed to snuggle closer within his arms and rest her head against his chest. He seemed in a reflective mood and didn't attempt any conversation as they moved around the floor.

The evening wore on, and she forced herself to sparkle appreciative among the others, but the effort was tiring and she would have given almost anything to have been able to ask Cesare to take her back to their motel suite.

When Marcello politely asked her to dance after supper, she accepted with a slight smile, trying to mask her weariness. They had barely moved part of the way round the floor when she saw Cesare and Francesca leave the table. It was all she could do not to cry out with an anguish so real it was a physical ache as Francesca moved into Cesare's arms, complementing his magnificent stature perfectly. Marisa could not tear her eyes away as Cesare bent his head to listen attentively to whatever Francesca appeared to be uttering seductively into his ear. She felt a sickening jealousy rise from the depth of her being, and was so infuriated, if perchance Marcello had spoken she would have been hard put to it not to snap his head right off in her rage. The cheek of it, the utter and complete gall of the situation occurred shortly afterwards in the powder room where both she and Francesca repaired simultaneously.

A brief desolate glimpse in the mirror reflected the comparison between them only too clearly. She looked a pale insignificant shadow compared with the other girl. Her make-up was simple, whereas Francesca's resembled a glossy advertisement for an exclusive brand of cosmetics applied with the skill of a beautician.

Marisa patted powder on to her shiny nose, and proceeded to find fault with her every visible physical attribute. 'Too short, too pale, eyes too large for my face, mouth too wide, a tip-tilted nose, and my hair is——' Her self-criticism was interrupted as Francesca turned slightly towards her and paused in the midst of applying perfume to her wrists.

'You'll forgive me if I express curiosity, and enquire how you happened to meet Cesare?' Her voice was cool, but her eyes were far from indifferent.

Marisa concentrated on fixing a stray wisp of hair and forced a smile to her lips. 'I had a puncture, miles away from anywhere, and was changing the tyre when Cesare stopped to help me.'

Francesca raised an elegant eyebrow. 'How opportune! You worked in Mareeba?'

'No. In Mossman, doing secretarial work.' Marisa

gathered her evening bag and stood politely waiting for the other girl.

Francesca's eyes narrowed speculatively. 'You knew, of course, that Cesare and I have been very close friends for some considerable time?'

Marisa's stomach lurched. How close was *close*? With commendable dignity she looked Francesca squarely in the eye. 'I think we'd better get back, don't you?'

A pitiless laugh left Francesca's lips as she collected her cosmetics together and slid them carelessly into her bag. 'You foolish *child*! You surely don't imagine *you* can hold him?'

Marisa longed to turn and leave, to step through the door into the gay chattering crowd only yards away, and there was nothing to stop her. Afterwards, she could not have said who gave her the courage to speak as she did, nor which guardian angel happened to be smiling down on her at the time. Had she been an actress, her performance would have won an award, she felt sure.

'Francesca,' she began calmly, 'I'm sorry you feel bitter about my marriage. As you are such a *close* friend of Cesare's, you will know he would never be coerced into marriage. His past is his own, I have no claim on that,' she concluded quietly.

Francesca shot her a venomous glare and brushed past to the door, fury evident in every action.

Marisa's serene façade collapsed, and it took all her resources not to give way to childish tears. However could she go out there now and pretend nothing had happened?

It took a few agonising minutes to summon the will to open the door. The noise rumbled and bubbled about her, and the softly lit air was heavy with the aroma of cigars and the occasional fragrance of an exotic perfume.

As she sat down she breathed an inaudible sigh, relieved that her legs had not collapsed beneath her as they had threatened to, at least once, during the seemingly endless distance back to the table. Rafaella and

Ottorino were drinking coffee, and Cesare cast her a swift penetrating glance as he poured some of the steaming liquid into a cup for her.

Of Francesca and Marcello there was no sign, fortunately, for she felt drained and emotionally incapable of pursuing a verbal battle. Mercifully, Cesare took the initiative to leave, and only when they were in the car did she relax and let the sleepiness she had held at bay steal over her.

Two evenings later, Marisa emerged from their bedroom into the lounge attired in white crimplene slacks and a gaily patterned tunic in shades of lilac and pink. Her hair fell loosely about her shoulders and her feet were clad in cork-heeled sandals.

They were almost ready to leave for a barbecue at the Donatis', and she felt a purely primitive thrill at the sight of Cesare standing so tall and broad, at ease as he patiently waited for her to join him. She wanted to fling her arms around him and lift her face to his, but she didn't possess the courage to take the initiative. She knew he was fond of her, but somehow mere affection no longer seemed sufficient.

'Penny for them?' he questioned lightly, moving to her side.

Marisa smiled, forcing her voice to sound cheerful. 'Nothing really, just wondering how Tony is getting on,' she offered, feeling guilty that up until this moment she hadn't thought of him at all.

He caught her chin between his fingers and lifted her face to his, looking down at the light smudges beneath her eyes. 'You're looking pale, do you feel tired?'

Her lashes swept upwards, and she saw the concern for her in his expression and shook her head.

'A little, but not sleepy-tired, just a can't-be-bothered-very-much sort of tired.'

He touched the tip of her nose with his lips, commenting they would not stay too late. 'This is meant to be a holiday, not a social whirl. I have no intention of letting you arrive back at Mareeba tired and in need of a rest,' he said severely.

Well, that was nice. At least he noticed, she mused, as a warm glow spread inside her, and she found courage to ask about the Donati family, lightly including Francesca in her query.

She missed the instant flicker of comprehension in his eyes, and by the time she looked up at him his expression was an inscrutable mask.

'Ottorino is a cousin by marriage to my father,' he began impassively. 'Years ago, when you would scarcely have been out of the schoolroom, my mother, in one of her letters to Rafaella, fondly expressed the desire that Francesca and I should marry. In their own quiet way they've never given up.'

Relief flooded through her veins, leaving her giddy with joy. 'Oh,' she breathed thankfully. 'Then——?'

'No, my jealous infant,' he interrupted mockingly, 'I had never entertained the idea of *marriage* with Francesca. A beautiful untouchable ornament is not my ideal of a wife,' he finished inexorably.

The barbecue was a splendidly elegant affair, so totally unlike any barbecue Marisa had ever been to before. There was every kind of meat imaginable from a sucking pig roasting on a spit to chickens rotissiered by the dozens, accompanied by salads of every description, hot crunchy bread rolls, risottos lying resplendent in bowls beside side-plates of cold tongue, ham, beef, salami, and at least four different assorted cheeses. It was a riot of food, arranged elegantly to be eaten out of doors. Marisa felt ashamed at an inordinate longing for slightly burnt sausages on a stick held over a smoky fire, a slice of toasted bread and a mug of hot coffee.

She felt relaxed and happy as she danced with Marcello, then some Lothario by the name of Luigi who seemed to ignore the rings on the third finger of her left hand and was intent on proving how irresistible he was. Secretly she was rather amused at his outrageous flattery.

Francesca managed to commandeer Cesare for one of the rare dances that were slow enough to necessitate any contact with a partner, and Marisa felt her heart jolt at the sight of them. Francesca was very tall, and there was no doubt they looked a handsome pair.

After supper, Marisa drank a little more champagne than perhaps she should have; spent twenty minutes in the bathroom feeling horribly ill, wishing she could be sick but hoping she wouldn't. Finally she went in search of black coffee, discovered the kitchen, and was commiserated with by a maid and given a couple of tablets which helped considerably.

It was there that Cesare found her, a severe frown she could not discern as anger or worry creasing his forehead.

'What is wrong? Are you not feeling well?' he asked searchingly in carefully controlled tones.

She sipped the hot coffee pleasurably, feeling better by the minute.

'I did feel rather ill for a while, but the coffee seems to have helped,' she explained, looking suddenly repentant. 'I'm sorry, I should have told you, but at the time you were dancing with Francesca, and it seemed more important to get away in case I really *was* ill.'

Cesare looked down at her through narrowed eyes as he lit a cigarette. 'Are you sure you're all right?' He regarded her intently, and as she acquiesced, albeit faintly, firmly indicated his intention to take her home to the motel.

Once in the car, she leaned back against the seat and closed her eyes, not opening them till the car drew in beside their suite. Oh dear, her stomach did feel a bit peculiar, not her own at all, and once inside, she made straight for the bathroom and was horribly, violently ill.

'Oh, dear God!' she cried silently as the tears rolled down her cheeks. Finally, feeling wretchedly like a well-wrung rag, she realised the attack was over and slowly and thoroughly she washed her face and scrubbed her teeth with a liberal dob of toothpaste.

When she came back into the bedroom, Cesare was standing at the foot of the bed with a face like a thunder-cloud. She had never seen him so angry, and when he smote his fist into the palm of his hand, she jumped with fright.

With a muted growl, he let out a string of expletives which would have quailed anything and everything in sight. As it was she could only stand there, eyes wide, her pale face becoming paler with every passing second. The tirade came to an abrupt end with another fist-smiting action, and with anger evident in every line of his face he strode towards her menacingly.

His fury was the living end, and choking back a sob she turned and ran towards the door of the bedroom. She hadn't moved two steps when hard fingers gripped her arm and spun her round. Instinctively she put up a hand to cover her face, fearfully unsure of his intention.

'*Marisa!*' Shock was plain in his voice, and seconds later he pulled her into his arms, holding her against him.

It seemed several minutes before she could bear to look up at him. Two great tears spilled over and ran down her cheeks as she looked disconsolately up into his granite-like face. He swore briefly and explicitly before bending his head, his lips touching her forehead with a gentleness that caused the tears to flow more than ever. He held her then, letting her cry out the uncertainty, the fear, until she quietened and rested against him, timidly winding her arms round his waist. His lips found her hair, the lobe of her ear, the lids of her eyes, and the curve of her cheek before claiming her mouth in a kiss which melted her bones and made her want to cry all over again.

He flicked her nose with a stray finger and said softly. 'Tomorrow, *carina,* we are going to pack our bags and fly back to Cairns to spend five or six days on Green Island. Now, off to bed with you.'

Over breakfast next morning, he looked up and smiled, his dark eyes enquiring as they regarded her.

'Feeling better?'

Marisa nodded, adding, 'Much better, thank you.'

Green Island was exactly as she remembered, and they spent almost a week soaking up the sun and relaxing lazily on that idyllic atoll paradise.

As they drove up the gravel side-road to the farm, Marisa gave a sigh of contentment and stretched her arms. What a wonderful feeling to come *home*!

CHAPTER THIRTEEN

Rosa and Carlo left on Monday with the children for their holiday at Port Douglas. The children had only a fortnight's vacation from school and it seemed very quiet without them.

Cesare intended extending the acreage of tobacco, and bush on the western side of the farm had to be cleared, tree stumps pulled out, and all the new ground ploughed. There were over a hundred chicks due to be railed up from Cairns, Cesare informed her a few days after their return, and it would be beneficial if she were to begin killing and freezing at least half the existing poultry. The ducks too, as fifty-odd ducklings were due by rail as well. *And*, Marisa did realise, didn't she, that much of the vegetables in the garden should be pickled and stored ready for use during the coming season? Marisa wondered wryly whatever had made her think she might have a great deal of spare time!

Soccer training had begun, and each Sunday there was a game, either in Mareeba or Cairns.

Rosa and Carlo had been back from their holiday for little over a month when the telephone exchange put through an overseas call early after dinner. Cesare took it, and almost immediately whitened beneath his tan. Marisa stood by apprehensively as he spoke quietly and decisively, even soothingly on occasion, for all of ten minutes before replacing the receiver. He gave her no chance to speak as he checked the telephone directory for a number and then dialled it almost immediately, speaking rapidly and emphatically in his own language and lighting a cigarette with one hand as he did so. His face had tautened into a harsh, almost savage expression when at last he put down the phone and turned towards her.

'That was Isabella, my sister,' he said wearily as he raked an impatient hand through his hair. 'There has been a car accident, in which my father was killed instantaneously. Mamma is critically injured in hospital, and not expected to live more than a few days.'

Marisa felt her throat constrict with sorrow, and all she could find to say was, 'Cesare——' in a tiny hushed voice, her face almost as pale as his.

He stood silently, moving only as he lifted the cigarette to and from his mouth, and his quietness was enervating. She wished he would swear, or crash his fist down on to the table ... *anything*.

'I must go, *nina*,' he said at last. 'I am the only son, my place is there, until it is over. I cannot,' he continued, his eyes clouded with pain, 'leave it to my sister alone.'

Marisa opened her mouth to speak, and the words came out inarticulately as she strove to reassure him. 'Of course—yes. I'm so sorry—it's a terrible thing to have happened. Cesare, what can I *say*?' she finished brokenly, covering her face with trembling hands as the tears spilled over and ran down her cheeks.

'Shh, child, don't cry,' he raked a hand through his hair with an impatient gesture, regarding her with something akin to vexation. 'Marisa,' he cajoled inflexibly, pausing only for a few seconds before pulling her into his arms and holding her closely against him. 'Hush, *nina*,' he murmured gently. 'I must leave before dawn in the morning. The day after tomorrow, I will be at the hospital. Now,' he brushed his lips against the top of her head and gave her a light shake. 'Get some clothes together for me while I see Carlo, hmm?'

Marisa nodded numbly, and when he returned a little over an hour later she had all of the clothes she thought he would need folded neatly on the bed.

'Carlo will drive me down to Cairns,' he said fairly brusquely, tossing a suitcase on to the bed and rapidly filling it with clothes. 'I've signed a number of cheques for your use while I'm away.'

'Yes,' Marisa said quietly as she fingered the brocade of the bedspread.

He looked at her compellingly, snapping the locks on the suitcase and softening slightly as he saw her woebegone expression. 'I won't write, Marisa, but I will ring through after I've seen Mamma at the hospital.'

She nodded her head slowly, thinking how lonely the house would be without him, and *dear God,* how much she would miss him. It was a major effort of self-control not to burst into tears.

The first opalescent tinge of a new day was gently spreading over the deep blue-black sky as Cesare bent his head and kissed her hard on the lips. Then he gathered up his baggage and walked straight out of the house, without once looking back.

The tears trickled down her face unheeded as she watched the probing headlights of Carlo's station-wagon disappear from view.

Time dragged slowly while Cesare was away, and Marisa lived each waking hour as if it were a day until his call came. Oh, the bliss at the sound of his voice! It was a few minutes after eight in the morning, three days after he had left, and she flew to the telephone, lifting it with her heart thudding against her ribs.

'Yes,' she answered eagerly to the girl at the telephone exchange. 'Yes!' and then Cesare's voice came on the line.

'Marisa?'

'Yes.' she said for the third time, clutching the receiver tightly.

'Speak up, child, I can hardly hear you,' he commanded, and she swallowed and smiled, and wept, all at the same time.

'Cesare, it's so good to hear from you,' she managed after a few seconds. 'Did you have a good trip? How is your mother?' she queried hesitantly, brushing the tears from her lashes.

'Mamma is very bad, *nina,*' he answered with constraint. 'The doctors say the end cannot be far away.

She is unconscious, mercifully, and I will stay at the hospital until it is all over.'

Marisa nodded her head swiftly, and spoke into the telephone. 'You must be very tired.' Her voice was compassionate.

'A little,' he replied, and she could imagine him shrugging indifferently, as if it were of no account. 'And you, *nina*? You are eating well, not making do with coffee and toast for every meal? I do not wish to see you have lost weight when I return.'

'No—I mean yes,' she smiled into the phone. 'I'm fine,' she assured him confidently, thrilled that he should be concerned for her, especially now, when he must be grieving over his parents' tragedy.

'I must go, Marisa, you understand? I will ring again in a few days. *Ciao, nina.*'

'Yes. *Ciao,*' she answered, but he had already replaced the receiver and did not hear her. She put the phone down with a heartfelt sigh and looked around the spotlessly clean house, wondering what she could do to occupy herself.

That's it, she concluded with elation at a sudden thought. Wool—she would go into Mareeba and get some wool and knit Cesare a jersey. It would keep her occupied in the afternoons and evenings, and if she bought double knitting wool there was a chance she might have it finished by the time he returned.

It was Rosa, dear friendly good-natured woman that she was, who first indicated that Marisa's loss of appetite and apparent paleness could be due to something other than Cesare being away. From the first, she had insisted that Marisa eat her evening meal with them. It was, she had indicated philosophically, just as easy to cook for six as it was for five. Besides, her conscience would not allow her, nor Carlo's either, to enjoy their food knowing that she was sitting alone in that big house.

'It is possible you are with child, Marisa?' she enquired gently as they sat over morning coffee in Marisa's kitchen, well into the second week of Cesare's absence.

Marisa cast her a startled glance, opening her mouth to deny it. 'I don't—think so,' she said slowly with a frown of concentration as she tried to pinpoint a date, reflecting that it couldn't have been *that* long surely? There was a fleeting change of emotions in her expression as comprehension dawned that . . . *of course*! Why hadn't it occurred to her before?

'I think I might be,' she spoke softly, a rosy glow spreading over her face as her eyes sparkled across the table to Rosa. '*Si*,' nodded Rosa knowledgeably. 'It is right, that now Cesare lose his pappa and mamma, you are with child,' she finished with satisfaction.

'I'll go into Mareeba tomorrow to see the doctor,' Marisa said with conviction. 'Then I can be sure when the baby is due. Cesare said last night that his mother's funeral is tomorrow, and that it would be another week to ten days before he could leave. I—do you think I should tell him over the telephone, or wait until he gets home?' she asked Rosa anxiously.

Rosa spread her hands indecisively, then gave a shake of her head. 'I think maybe it be better to wait until he gets home,' she advised.

The visit to the doctor confirmed that come mid-December she would be a proud mama, and Marisa almost sang as she drove back to the farm. It was a sore temptation not to spill the news to Cesare when he rang the following week to say he would be flying out from Rome the next day.

'I'll be in Cairns on Wednesday evening on the Ansett flight—you will meet me?' his voice commanded deeply.

As if there was a chance she wouldn't! She would have been sorely indignant if he had insisted that Carlo drive down to collect him. Indeed! He'd been away almost a month, and she had missed him desperately. The mere thought that he would be home in a few days sent her heart soaring like a bird newly released from its cage into a beautiful park of tall broad-spreading green-leafed trees.

She baked all his favourite things—an apple shortcake, the light fruit cake he was particularly partial to, and some coconut biscuits. The house was polished and shining like a new pin, and all day Wednesday she fidgeted, unable to settle to a solitary thing. The flight time she had checked twice, and changed her mind over what to wear at least three times by the time she left the farm shortly after six o'clock. It was slightly less than an hour and a half's drive, but she couldn't stay in the house a moment longer.

As it was, she drove carefully and took her time, and still had more than half an hour to fill in at the airport. She sat and leafed through numerous magazines, but couldn't have said what was in them for the life of her.

The whine of the jet's engines set the nerves in her stomach tingling, and as she anxiously searched the faces descending from the plane, her chest was so tight she could scarcely breathe.

At last she saw him, striding head and shoulders above almost everyone else as he came towards the reception lounge, and it took all her strength to wait quietly behind the barrier.

As he came into the light, she almost gasped out loud at how tired and strained he looked. In that crowd of milling people, she was aware only of him, and she took the few steps necessary on winged feet straight into his arms. His lips met hers hungrily, and she returned his kiss unashamedly with a fervour that set his eyes gleaming darkly as he held her away.

'I—it's good to see you,' she said shakily, unable to take her eyes from his beloved face.

'You are looking well, *carina,*' he observed, smiling as he took her arm and led the way to collect his luggage.

She longed to blurt out her news there and then, and all the way to Mareeba she had to contain herself severely, schooling herself to be patient and wait until they were home. It was so wonderful that he was here, home at last, and as the car sped swiftly up on to the tableland, she could have shouted out loud with joy.

Carlo and Rosa opened their door as the car swept into the yard, and came out to welcome him home.

'Ah, my friends, it is good to be home,' Cesare assured them, accepting a friendly slap on the shoulder from Carlo.

'Come, you come inside and have coffee, it is all ready,' Rosa bade them quietly.

'*Grazie*, Rosa,' Cesare acknowledged, placing an arm round Marisa's shoulder, tucking her in to his side as they walked the short distance to Rosa's kitchen.

'Sit down, sit down,' Rosa gestured to them as she adjusted the percolator on the stove, and Carlo went to the cupboard and withdrew a bottle of brandy to lace their coffee.

The men leaned on the table and took a nip each of the brandy as Carlo informed Cesare of the details of the last tobacco sale. By that time Rosa had poured the coffee, and Marisa sat in her chair quite content to listen as she sipped the steaming brew.

It was more than an hour before Cesare rose to his feet, unfolding his length slowly and thrusting his hands into his trouser pockets as he uttered his thanks.

'You go on ahead, Marisa,' he bade, as they left Carlo's house. 'I must get my things from the car first.'

She nodded, making her way across the yard to their home, unlocking the door and turning on the lights. Cesare followed a few minutes later and slung his luggage straight through into their bedroom, shrugging off his suit jacket and loosening his tie.

'Open that suitcase, Marisa,' he instructed, unbuttoning his shirt and pulling it loose from inside his trousers. 'I must have a shower, but while I do, there are some things inside there for you. By the time you have found them I shall be back.'

'Yes,' she said dutifully in a small voice, and put the suitcase he had indicated on to the linen chest. As she unclasped the catch and lifted the lid, a hand reached out and ruffled her hair, then he was gone from the room.

Curiously she unpacked the suitcase to find several packages lying neatly at the bottom, and with trembling fingers she began opening them. There were tears in her eyes as she realised they had been his mother's, and she gave a strangled sob at the heartache it must have caused both him and Isabella to have gone through their parents' possessions. By the time she undid the fifth package, tears fell unchecked down her cheeks.

'Marisa,' Cesare chastised her quietly from behind, pulling her back against him as he bent his head to caress her hair. 'Don't cry, little one,' he said in a voice that was ragged with suppressed emotion, and convulsively she turned and flung herself into his arms, burying her head against his chest as she wound her arms tightly round his waist.

'Cesare,' she cried brokenly as she hugged him to her. 'They're so beautiful,' she whispered as his hands untied the ribbon at the nape of her neck, releasing her hair to sway softly in a shining cloud about her shoulders.

'Hush, *carina*. Don't talk now.' His breath was warm as his mouth fastened on hers, kissing her deeply as his fingers sought the fastenings on her clothes, releasing them from her unhurriedly until the last wisp was divested and lay at her feet. Her skin was soft and warm, and as intoxicating to his touch as a heady sweet wine.

'Oh, Cesare,' she whispered rapturously as he drew her down on to the bed, and she was swept away on the tide of his passion.

She slept curled into him, and enfolded against his warm body she nestled until he stirred in the early morning and gathered her to him, his caresses rousing her into awareness.

It was then she told him about the baby, her voice hesitantly shy in the semi-darkness of the room.

His arms tightened around her and he murmured, 'Are you pleased?' against her ear in such a way she knew he was not altogether surprised at her news.

'I—I'm thrilled ... but you're not surprised—how could you know?'

His mouth fastened on hers as he kissed her gently. 'I had my suspicions when we were on holiday, *carina*,' he enlightened her quietly.

Marisa did some swift mental calculations. 'As long ago as that?' she queried with surprise, and he chuckled against her throat and sank his teeth gently into the lobe of her ear.

'As long ago as that,' he confirmed lightly. 'Never mind, *nina,* after the third or fourth little *bambino* you can surprise me, hmmn?'

'Oh, you——!' she began, wriggling to escape his grasp and failing hopelessly. His lips met hers demandingly, and she clung to him achingly, lost in the rapture of his lovemaking.

Pregnancy suited her. She positively glowed with good health and well-being, marvelling at the feel of the child within her. With maternal devotion, she began collecting nappies, little gowns and jackets, never ceasing to wonder at the miracle of nature. Cesare regarded her with indulgence, and she smiled at the whole world as she basked in the warmth of his affection.

As she stood on a chair in the room she had chosen to use as a nursery, reaching out to adjust the new curtains she had that moment finished hanging, she never in her wildest imagination thought she might over-balance and fall awkwardly to the floor. The piercing pain in her ribs cut her breathing, and she could manage little more than a hoarse whisper trying to call out to anyone who might possibly hear her.

'Oh, God,' she cried brokenly, 'don't let my baby die.' The tears streamed down her face as she willed the baby to move; a slight flutter would do, *anything* to let her know she was safe. She tried to move, to struggle to her feet somehow, and after many minutes of manoeuvring she was able to manage it at last. The telephone was her only hope, as Cesare and Carlo were out in the paddock, and Rosa had gone into town only ten minutes before. With shaking fingers she dialled the Petricevics' number, praying that someone was inside the house to answer the telephone. It rang and rang, and then mercifully the receiver was lifted.

'Hallo?' It sounded like Gianna's voice, and Marisa sobbed her name.

'Gianna, is that you?' clutching the receiver agonisingly.

'*Si*, who is there?' she queried anxiously.

'Gianna, it's Marisa. Marisa Gianelli,' Marisa cried desperately. 'Can you come over and get Cesare from the paddock? Please!' she urged pleadingly as she began to shake uncontrollably. 'I fell off a chair, and there's no one here. I only just made it to the telephone,' she finished on a heartbroken sob, and Gianna's voice instantly became matter-of-fact.

'Yes, right away.' The phone went dead, and Marisa steadily made her way towards the nearest chair and sat down gingerly to wait.

It seemed an eternity before a car sped into the yard, carrying on through to the track running down to the paddock where Cesare and Carlo were shifting pipes to water the young tobacco. Several minutes later the car roared back and doors slammed as Cesare hurried into the house with Gianna close behind him.

Marisa couldn't even cry, it hurt so much, and big tears welled up in her eyes and spilled over, one by one, sliding down her cheeks as Cesare lifted her gently and carried her out to the car. Gianna patted her hand consolingly and uttered a few sympathetic words of encouragement, then Cesare put the car in motion and drove it swiftly to the hospital.

The next few hours were a blur as particulars were taken and she was put into a bed, to be examined first by a nursing Sister and a little while later by a doctor. To her stricken queries about the baby, he would only comment—'We shall see, we shall see.'

Cesare came into the room straight after that and sat with her, but she could not look at him for fear of finding some hint of reproach in his face. In a way she was relieved when he left, for her throat felt so dry and constricted with fear she couldn't have uttered one word if her life had depended upon it.

She did not remember a great deal, things were very hazy in between the waves of pain. She thought she saw Cesare's face bending over her on more than one occasion, but couldn't have been sure.

The haze cleared gradually, and she opened her eyes and looked round the room hesitantly, conscious that she seemed to hurt most everywhere. Her head swung towards the door as it opened.

'Oh good, you are awake. How are you feeling?' the nurse queried breezily, popping a thermometer into Marisa's mouth and taking hold of her wrist as she checked her pulse. 'Do you feel like something to eat? A cup of tea, perhaps?'

Marisa mumbled that tea would be just fine. There was a saline drip attached to her right wrist, and it felt a little odd. Curious to know whether it was morning or afternoon, she asked when her tea was brought in, and was amazed to discover she had been in hospital three days.

The doctor called in soon after, and it was then she learnt the baby had been a little girl, and that at five months she had been too premature to survive. There was no reason, he continued, why she shouldn't have another child, in fact he advised her to have another as soon as possible,

Cesare visited each evening, and although she looked forward all day to seeing him, her efforts at conversation were desultory. She felt heartbroken, and had the terrible empty feeling that any hope she had of holding Cesare's affection was lost. Worse, in the knowledge that it was all her own fault, accident or no.

Rosa called in almost every afternoon, and Gianna, Luisa, Anna and Elena took it in turns to visit every few days. There were lots of visitors, she was never an afternoon without at least two.

At the end of ten days she left the hospital with the admonition to take things easy for a few weeks, and to report back in a month.

Cesare drove her home, and apart from a monosyllabic 'yes' or 'no', she sat in silent apathy, unable to raise her low spirits.

The house was bright and shining, and she knew she

had Rosa to thank. She even managed a weak smile, and gave her a quick hug in gratitude, refusing further help politely.

'You've been marvellous, Rosa. Thanks a million, but I'm fine now, really I am,' she assured her brightly.

Rosa caught a glance from Cesare and offered to call over later, and when she had gone down the steps, he lit a cigarette and leaned against the edge of the table.

'We've two men starting tomorrow, do you think you can cope?' he queried as he blew smoke over one shoulder.

'Of course,' Marisa answered politely, not able to look at him.

His eyes narrowed slightly as he regarded her. 'I'm picking them up from town this afternoon. You had better check if there's anything you need, and give me a list.'

She fingered the material of her skirt absently, and nodded.

Cesare let out an exclamation of impatience. 'For God's sake, Marisa,' he bit out angrily, running a hand through his hair, but at the sight of her trembling lip and downcast head, he moved to stand in front of her. 'Look, it's over, nothing can change that,' he said gently, lifting her chin so that she had to look at him.

She blinked, trying hard not to cry as he bent and kissed her hard on the mouth, then he pinched her cheek lightly as he straightened up.

'No more tears, *nina,*' he bade sternly, and she shook her head, unable to speak for the constriction in her throat as he left.

CHAPTER FOURTEEN

THOSE first few weeks were difficult, to say the least.

Marisa threw herself into a spring-cleaning spree which she kidded herself was necessary, and declined any effort on Cesare's part to go visiting, or even to go into town to the cinema on a Saturday night. She hated the thought of reading pity in the eyes of those who would seek to reassure her, and express their sympathy.

She tried out elaborate new dishes, and baked until she had every conceivable tin filled with cakes and biscuits. Then she turned her attention feverishly to the garden, and not content, dug a border round the entire house and planted numerous shrubs and flower seedlings. At the end of each day she felt worn out and characterless. Her appetite had faded away to practically nothing, and she existed on fruit juice and the odd few morsels of food she forced down her throat each mealtime.

Towards Cesare, she was especially polite and courteous, not spontaneous and friendly in her usual sparkling fashion. Cesare's temper, hitherto held carefully in check, exploded somewhat when she intimated that she did not wish to visit the Petricevic family for dinner the following Sunday.

'In heaven's name, why not?' he ground out furiously, and his brow creased ominously. 'You can't hide in the house forever! I've accepted their invitation, and you *are* coming.' he finished with relative quietness.

Marisa felt the prick of tears, and raised a hand in silent entreaty. 'I just don't feel like facing anyone yet,' she began tentatively.

'*Madonna mia!*' he swore decisively, throwing his hands heavenward. 'It has been five weeks now! What am I to do with you? *Dio santo!* I have tried to be patient with you. How long is this to go on?' He crashed his fist down on to the table, berating her. 'You are not the only woman ever to have lost a child!'

Marisa put her hands over her ears. 'Stop it, stop yelling at me,' she implored, her eyes so large they seemed to fill her face.

'I am not yelling!' he exclaimed brusquely.

'You are,' she cried brokenly, rubbing her eyes. 'You—you should have married someone else—someone l-like Tania,' she bit out childishly. 'I'm sure she w-wouldn't be as—st-stupid as I am, and—and *cry* over ev-*everything*. She wouldn't do cr-crazy things like standing on a chair when she was pregnant!' She burst into tears and ran into the hall to their bedroom, slamming the door behind her.

She leant back against it, biting her lip in remorse. Oh, dear heaven, *what had she done*!

The door-handle twisted, and Cesare rapped loudly on the door. 'Get away from the door, Marisa, or by heaven, I'll push it in!' he threatened tautly.

But an icy sort of fatalism settled in her bones and she could not move. She felt the door being pushed from the outside, and Cesare's voice dangerously quiet as he warned her to stand aside. Silently she moved, watching in fearful fascination as he walked into the room. Every visible muscle tautened formidably as he sought control. He glared down at her for several seconds, his eyes glittering dangerously as his hands clenched and unclenched at his side, then he turned and strode from the room, out of the house, and seconds later she heard the car start and speed swiftly from the yard down the gravel driveway.

Unrestrained, she flung herself on to the bed and sobbed her heart out for a very long time. It seemed all the trials and sorrows over the past ten years were accounted for. At some stage of the night she stirred, feeling cold, and dazedly changed into her nightgown before sliding in between the sheets.

She did not hear the car come back, and when she woke in the morning Cesare had not slept beside her. Her head pounded and her stomach was tied up in knots with nervous tension, but she prepared breakfast stoically, determined to carry on as usual.

Cesare came in with the workers, and sat down at the table looking stern and formidable. The men seemed to sense that something was afoot and ate their meal as quickly as they decently could, rising to their feet and tucking in their chairs before disappearing from the kitchen. Cesare soon followed them, not reappearing until lunch-time, which was a disaster of a meal conversationally as it was eaten in complete silence.

At dinner she gave up trying to think of something

to say, and pushed the food around her plate feeling that if she put any of it into her mouth she would surely choke. There was nothing apparent to claim his attention after dinner, no barns to check, no tobacco to sort in the bulking shed, and she was sure Cesare would stay in the house. But she was mistaken, for he left the dining-room with the workers, disappearing across the yard to Carlo's house.

She was already in bed when he returned much later, and she waited with bated breath for him to come into the room, and could have cried with mortification when she heard the spare bedroom door close. She wished fervently that she had the courage to slip out of bed and go to him, to apologise and beg his leniency and understanding.

Another day passed in silence, and yet another. He seemed a stranger, and she couldn't bear it. She longed to talk to him quietly and rationally, to have the chance to explain she loved him so much it was a physical pain to be apart from him like this. The loss of their child didn't matter, there would be other children to follow. Couldn't he understand she needed reassurance and his love—yes, *love*—as desperately as a parched plant needed water?

She rehearsed in her mind what she would say, how she would say it, until it was indelibly printed in her brain, and she determined when next he came into the house she would have it out with him. But her courage withered and died at the cool, impersonal expression on his face, and her carefully memorized apology remained unuttered.

Next morning, after breakfast, she made up her mind, and it seemed as she did so, a cold hand clutched her heart and squeezed the life-blood out from it. She couldn't stay any longer, so close and yet so very far apart from him. He didn't love her, he couldn't. She was nothing more to him than an affectionate pet, obedient to his every command. It was impossible to go on like this, she told herself as she packed a suitcase with only a few of her clothes. She would drive the car into Mareeba in time to get the mid-afternoon train down to Cairns, then take the evening rail-car to Brisbane.

Luckily, it was Rosa's smoko that afternoon, and at fifteen minutes past two Marisa slipped her one suitcase on to the back seat of the car and drove swiftly from the yard. At the railway station she parked the car and locked it, passing the keys in to the stationmaster for safekeeping. He eyed her curiously, but laboriously wrote out a label for 'Cesare Gianelli' and tied it on to the key-ring before tossing it on to a shelf behind him.

In the carriage, Marisa stared sightlessly out of the window, looking every bit as heartbroken and forlorn as she felt. The words—'running away, you're running away' echoed and re-echoed in her mind, and she was emotionally and physically drained by the time the train pulled into Cairns two and a half hours later.

The station platform revealed few stragglers waiting as she alighted from the train, and she supposed she should get something to eat, but the thought of food choked her, and even a cup of hot coffee didn't rouse sufficient interest to warrant making the effort of going to get it.

What Cesare's reaction would be when he found her gone sent shivers of apprehension up and down her spine, and the enormity of what she had done began to magnify itself into alarming proportions. She swayed on her feet, suddenly unable to stand. She must sit down, otherwise she would fall down, she thought rather hysterically.

Strong hard fingers curled round her arm, and her heart lurched crazily as she turned to see Cesare regarding her with anger evident in every line of his powerful frame.

She stamped her foot with frustration, and tried valiantly to free her arm from his excruciating grip.

'Oh, let me go, let me *go!*' she cried wretchedly, wrenching her arm futilely. 'I'm nothing to you,' she continued shakily, impatiently brushing away the hot tears blurring her vision. 'Nothing but—but a—an obliging housekeeper, and——' she gasped painfully as his fingers bit cruelly into her arm, wincing at his grim, muscle-tautened features.

He said nothing, his eyes blazing down into hers for timeless seconds before he led her along the platform and down the steps to the car.

As he drove through the traffic she felt a sense of rising panic, the desire to escape uppermost in her mind.

'I can't go back with you,' she said desperately, becoming alarmed as he turned the car into a motel entrance and halted in front of one of the rear units.

He turned slightly in his seat so that one elbow rested on the steering wheel, and he regarded her silently through narrowed eyes. His voice, although calm, held the hidden steel of an almost exhausted forbearance.

'I am entitled to an explanation, am I not?'

Marisa jumped visibly at the sound of his voice, and her answer was barely audible. 'I—yes, I guess so.'

'I was unaware of your absence until Carlo informed me at smoko-time that Rosa was worried something might be wrong as she had seen you put a suitcase into the car and drive away. I telephoned the railway station, and my suspicions were confirmed that you *had* taken the train—and, incidentally, that my car-keys were awaiting collection. It is as well,' he intoned ruthlessly, 'that my temper has had time to cool during the hour I have spent waiting for the train to arrive.' His fist clenched the steering wheel angrily, almost as if he wished it were a part of *her*. 'I have booked a room here.' He took the key from the ignition and slid out from the car, going round to the other side and opened her door. 'Marisa,' he cautioned carefully as he stood waiting, 'I am capable of carrying you if I have to.'

She slid from the seat just as he leaned forward to grasp her arms, and stood silently, smothering a cry of pain as he caught her forearm and propelled her forward.

Inserting a key into the lock of the door immediately in front of him, he led her inside the room.

'Now,' he demanded, his eyes glittering with suppressed fury as he glared down at her. 'You will tell me what this is all about!'

Marisa remained silent, unable to marshal her thoughts into any rational whole. 'I can't go home—go back, with you, I just *can't*!' she stumbled over the words, becoming angry with herself at her incoherence. 'You married me only because you wanted a housekeeper. You *said* so!' She twisted a lock of hair round her fingers nervously as she stared sightlessly around the room.

'And you are so much a child that you believe that now?' he queried inflexibly.

Marisa tugged at her hair crossly. 'I don't know. I don't! I never know what you mean. You don't *say* anything!' she burst out in anguish, completely perplexed and very close to tears. 'Why don't you let me go? I mean nothing to you. I'm just someone you amuse yourself with——' she broke off as hard hands lifted her off her feet and brought her close up against him. His eyes smouldered darkly, savagely, down into hers for one long minute, then his mouth descended on hers, punishing with its cruel intensity and she clutched blindly at him, trying to push against his chest, and failing hopelessly. She suffered the hard relentless pressure of his mouth until she gasped for breath, and when at long last he lifted his head she could only look up at him in reproach, her eyes drowning in the welled-up tears which threatened to spill over at any second.

'God help me, you deserved that!' he uttered in a dangerously quiet voice as he let his hands fall to his sides.

Marisa touched her painfully bruised lips with shaking fingers. 'Cesare, please,' she made a bewildered gesture as if asking impunity. 'You've been—so—so impatient with me since—lately,' she amended unsteadily. 'I was—am—so unsure of you. I tried to apologise, for b-being so childish, but you were so un-unapproachable,' the words tumbled out jerkily. 'You slept in the spare room,' she accused irrationally, tightly hugging her arms together as she felt herself begin to shake uncontrollably. Desperately she clasped her arms in an effort to still the feeling of despair that was rapidly encompassing her whole being. Nothing mattered any more.

When she didn't answer, his expression softened slightly, and he forced her chin between his fingers, lifting it until she had to meet his compelling gaze.

'Words, Marisa?' he questioned inexorably. 'You need *words*?'

Her lips trembled, and she felt her eyes fill with tears. Her control was almost at an end.

'*Dio Madonna*! Don't cry,' he groaned despairingly as he held her face between his hands.

She whispered brokenly, any vestige of pride gone. 'I love you. Always—always I've loved you.' She shut her eyes, trying to still the tears that were beginning to course down her cheeks.

A great heartfelt sigh left his lips, and he eased the tears away with gentle fingers, then gathered her close against him as he stroked her hair soothingly.

'Marisa, *inamorata*,' he whispered gently, kissing the tears away as they trickled down her face. 'It's all right, *cara*. Don't cry,' he begged as his lips sought hers, lingeringly with great tenderness, and when he lifted his head it was to look down with such a wealth of love in his eyes that she cried all over again.

'I love you, Marisa. More than life itself,' he revealed quietly. 'You bewitched me from that very first day we met. Such a slim young scrap of a girl, covered in dust and grease, and fairly spitting with anger when I stopped to help you.' He put a gentle finger to her lips, stilling her protest. 'It seemed almost fate when I learnt your name and address at the garage and realised you were my tenant. The Mini was already gone when I reached that relatively deserted stretch of road, although I could not have missed you by more than ten minutes,' he enlarged. 'When Mr Grieves duly reported the sad sorry tale I became very angry,' his voice deepened and he held her closer against him. 'I determined to make you see marriage to me was your only solution. Your tears, *carina*, before I declared my intention an honourable one, were almost my undoing, but I resolved to wait, to give you time to settle in on the farm, and hopefully to know me better. You were more than a little in awe of me, and such an innocent,' he bent his head and kissed her with a thoroughness that left her starry-eyed and breathless.

He took her face gently between his hands and she felt her throat constrict in wonder as his broad rawboned features softened miraculously.

'One lifetime will not be long enough, *cara mia*,' he vowed tenderly.

Marisa wound her arms up around his shoulders, revelling with joy at the way his arms tightened about her with unconcealed passion. His lips sought hers with a sensual expertise that sent the blood pulsing through her veins, and set her limbs trembling with a treacherous longing.

In the early dawn hours the car turned off the gravel road leading to the farm and came to rest under the verandah. As they walked across the yard towards the house Cesare's arm encircled her waist, drawing her close in to his side. Marisa smiled lovingly up at him and released a sigh of utter contentment. Together, hand in hand, they had come home.